Ramona's party had only begun…

"Get out. Get out my house of my house. Get out now!" Ramona yelled at the top of her voice as she chased the strange things out of the house using the broom alternately as a club or a baseball bat.

They kept on dancing and shouting, "Party! Party!" as they walked past her in a long conga line.

Her ears rang with the noise they made leaving which almost her deafened her.

She went into the kitchen and looked at Wayne who had gone back to the kitchen to finish putting the coffee cups away.

"Wayne, did you see that?" she said not trusting herself.

"See what? I heard a lot of loud music, but I thought it was just an alarm clock radio that went off." He went and let Susie out of the furnace room.

"No. We just had a bunch of three foot high cats and rats and elephants dancing in our living room," she said.

Wayne looked at her and nodded, but didn't say anything.

She stopped and went into the living room to see if there was any evidence of what she had seen.

THE DARK ZONE

Rita Schulz

Edited by R. Edgewood

Published by 53rd Street Publishing
Offices in Gibsons, B.C. Canada and Lincoln City,
Oregon

OTHER COLLECTIONS FROM RITA SCHULZ

THE DARK ZONE

Published by 53rd Street Publishing
Copyright 2015 Rita Schulz
All rights reserved

Cover art © Can Stock Photo Inc. / rolffimages
Print ISBN 978-1-927621-48-6

Edited by Colleen Kuehne
Cover designed by R. Edgewood
Cover design and layout © 2015 by 53rd Street
Publishing

53rd Street Publishing
Head office: Gibsons B.C. Canada
www.53rdstreetpublishing.com

CONTENTS

FORWARD

I'm always excited when I get the opportunity to put together a collection for one of our authors. I have been honored to bring you many stories by the talented, Rita Schulz.

Rita's voice in truly unique and often presents a different take on what it means to be human. In this collection she takes you to the moon in the far future, discovers very unique visitors from another dimension and faces the end of the world.

I hope you enjoy these stories as much as I have.

R. Edgewood
Managing Editor
53rd Street Publishing

INTRODUCTION

The end of the world has been depicted on film and in books since time began. The Bible has an entire book devoted to the end of the world.

On television popular shows such as Z Nation and The Walking Dead explore the zombie apocalypse.

Theatrical films such as A Boy and His Dog (derived from the story by the legendary Harlan Ellison), Escape from New York, and On The Beach have fostered a possible dark future ahead.

In his collection I explore the humanity behind the end of the world. Will we go down fighting or with a whimper? Do we have a choice?

These and other questions are explored in these stories and I have selected them for this very purpose.

Rita Schulz
November 2015

Rebellion

"Hi, I'm Erin. You must be, Tony," I said when a man approached wearing the uniform of the International Border and Immigration Service.

This was the first time we had actually met although we had been in touch by electronic mail.

I turned and looked up at the Earth. The dome wasn't completely clear, as I had thought it would be. It was tinted a bronze color, probably to filter out some of the sun's more deadly rays. It was amazing, seeing the Earth hanging in the ink-black sky like a big blue-and-white ball.

"Good guess. I'm Tony Eland; it's nice to meet you. You're Erin Thorne, I believe?" he said.

I nodded and we walked side by side into Elliot Space Station's town's warehouse. I smelled the cold wet of the cement and the grease and oil from the equipment and forklifts. There was also a hint of a pine scent reminiscent of wooden shipping crates.

Rebellion

There were a dozen self-contained domes on the moon. They were all pressurized and included artificial gravity—close to Earth normal—air and fresh water from the reclamation system augmenting the water mines on the dark side of the moon. This one was for the mining and processing of minerals that would be shipped to earth.

Suddenly shots rang out around us forcing me to dive for cover my heart racing. With the first shots, I dropped on the cement floor, rolled onto my belly, and sighted my pistol over the shoulder of Tony Eland, the man I was replacing on my moon assignment. I tightened my fingers around the smooth, hard grip of the gun and fired in the direction the shots had come from.

Interesting, the gun handled differently in the moon's low gravity: the kick wasn't as hard, but the bullet also didn't stay up as long and the trajectory different.

My heart started to pound and my mouth went dry as adrenalin flooded my system.

I smelled the acrid stench of fresh gunpowder, mingling with a damp mustiness coming from the warehouse.

The bullets pinged off the wooden crates and metal barrels stacked around them in this massive warehouse. The building was twice the length of one of Earth's football fields and a good three stories high. Bright lights hung from open metal scaffolding overhead, illumining the warehouse and its contents.

We were in the new warehouse area under a new dome next to a new space station, Elliot Space Station, so luckily everything around us was pressurized.

Huge crates—a few wood, but mostly metal—full of goods, surrounded us. Some consumer soft goods, some perishables, and some commercial goods that were destined to be components of homes and businesses; at least, that's what the shipping manifest said.

Another shot pinged above our heads. We both ducked and lay flat on the cold, dirty, greasy, cement floor.

"I'm going to get closer, cover me," I said to Tony.

He crawled closer toward me.

"What did you say, Erin?" asked the tall, dark man. Tony's head was shaved, but on his upper lip was a thick, neatly trimmed mustache.

His black pants and light blue shirt with the International Border and Immigration Service flash on both shoulders were clean and pressed. He obviously took pride in his appearance.

My uniform looked just like Tony's, only his fit better since he was a lean, six-foot male that the uniform had been designed for. The color was good for me; the blue was nice and suited my red hair. But I really hated trying to fit my five-feet-eight medium female body, curves and all, into a man's shirt and pants. It just didn't work.

"I said this isn't fair. This assignment was supposed to be like playing a round of golf, a walk in the park, a beautiful lunar vacation. So far, this has been a really lousy vacation." I crouched low and ran across the slippery cement floor.

Shots started and echoed in the large area. I tasted bile as the acid in my stomach tried to escape.

"A vacation? Where did you get that idea?" asked Tony in a loud voice as he rolled and came up next to a large metal barrel. He crouched and looked around the corner of the barrel to see where the shooters were hiding.

Everything went suddenly quiet.

Too quiet.

"The guy at the International Border Guard Recruitment Center on Earth told me this new station would be a piece of cake, like being on a holiday. I figured it would be a good first assignment for me."

I heard someone coming toward me. It sounded like heavy, size-fourteen work boots hitting the cement floor. Much like my ex-boyfriend's boots.

I dove, rolled over my shoulder, came up behind a medium, four-foot-high wooden crate, and fired in the direction of size fourteen.

"You did identify us when you went into the foreman's office, right?" I asked as I took a second to glance around us.

"I didn't go to the foreman's office. I thought you did. I just got here and met you at the door," said Tony as he squeezed of another couple of shots toward the sounds of the footsteps.

We heard something land with a thud on the cement.

"Do you think we should identify ourselves now?" I asked. Tony was the senior member of the team; I was waiting for him to take the lead.

I had been told by the Elliot Space Station people that he, Officer Eland, had been here for the last fifteen years while the station was built and knew who everybody was and where everything was kept.

"This is International Customs and Immigrations. Drop you weapons," yelled Tony. There was a shot punctuating the end of his sentence. As I watched, I saw Tony disappear behind a crate and not come up.

There was a massive barrage of gunfire. It sounded like it was coming from at least two different directions, but it was hard to tell.

"Do we know who these guys are?" I asked as a bullet whizzed close by my head. I flattened myself against the crate.

"No," answered Tony through clenched teeth. It sounded as if he were still to my right.

"Ah, you let them know that we were going to be working in here today?" I asked as I moved toward his hiding spot.

"No. I usually just walk over, say "hi" to whoever is working on the floor, and do my business. This is driving me nuts!" yelled Tony as the barrage of bullets increased, making conversation impossible.

I got to his side—he was on his butt, leaning against a crate—and knelt down. I saw that he had a wound on the top of his shoulder. It was bleeding. I motioned him to show me his arm and he shook his head. Then he handed me a strip of cloth that looked like it had come from the bottom of his shirt.

I tied it over his wound, then kissed my fingertips and touched the wound lightly.

"You'll be fine," I said softly, smiling at him.

He nodded at me. "Thanks."

"Okay, fellas, that's enough. You're in an enclosed dome. You have no place to run to and nowhere to hide. Give yourselves up," yelled Tony.

I quickly went back to my previous hiding place and waited for the next round of gunfire.

"I left a…" I started to say. Then I saw a red flash from the corner of my eye.

Next thing I knew, a tall, heavy-set man with a long, bushy beard came out from the six-foot-high metal drums with a long wrench raised in his hand. He was staring at me with anger and hatred.

I turned, karate-chopped his arm. The man grunted and dropped his weapon. It clattered on the cement as I kicked it away.

"Sir, face down, on the ground, now!" I commanded as I watched the man lie on the ground. I can't help but be polite, that how I was trained.

"Okay. Everyone, I have a loaded gun pointed at your friend's head. I need you all to come out and drop your weapons. Then we can talk about what's happening," I said as I tried to hold my gun steady and keep my hand from trembling.

Nothing happened. No one moved. There wasn't a sound in the warehouse.

I put my best poker face on, waiting for whoever was there to do what I'd told them to, because I didn't know what to do next. Then I realized that Tony wasn't there with me. Oh, great. Was he okay? He was hurt, but it hadn't looked that bad. Or had he left?

"Hold on. We're coming out," said a low male voice. I heard a few pairs of boots shuffling closer to me in the warehouse.

"Stand where I can see you and drop your weapons." I thought I'd say it again. If it worked the first time, maybe it would keep on working.

I heard something or someone behind me.

I turned, my gun in my hand, ready to fire. The person behind held up his hands. He was a small, thin, scared-looking man in his mid-twenties. His face was pale and his eyes were big and round.

What was happening in this place?

"Erin, I'm coming out," said Tony. He waited a moment, then stepped out from behind a wall of stacked boxes.

"Do you have cuffs? I don't have any yet."

"Yeah, that's nice. You just about blasted the boss." Tony looked at the young man standing there and smiled.

"Hi, George, you can put your arms down now…"

"Oh, I didn't know," I said. What was going on here?

"Sam, are you okay?" asked Tony, calling to the other person, on the floor waiting to be cuffed.

"What is this, a joke?" I asked, feeling my temper start to rise as I figured it out. Not a nice trick. I hated practical jokers.

"Of course. You can't expect to come into a place like Elliot Space Station, which is all of six buildings and about one-hundred-and-twenty people, and not expect a welcome of some sort," said Tony as he holstered his gun.

Tony reached into his shirt pocket and pulled out a small data pad. He keyed some information into it, and then handed it to me.

"Before we go on, could you please sign this for me? It's just a simple release form. Please read it, sign it, and I'll send it to the boss. You'll get a copy for your records, too," he said, handing me the pad.

I looked at it. He was right, it was simple. It said that I had arrived on Elliot Space Station and was now starting my job as an International Customs and Immigration officer. It looked right, so I signed it.

I heard voices and looked up.

There were a good dozen men, all different sizes, color, heights, and shapes, coming toward me. They were all wearing jeans and worn work shirts and they had one thing in common: they were all smiling. I got big hugs from some and pats on the back from others. Some had a lot of body odor and others smelled like cologne or a flower shop.

"Thank you. We're so glad you're here. Finally, we have something else to look at besides Tony's ugly mug," said one of the men, who sported interesting tattoos on his neck and had smelt very clean and nice.

"Come with me and I'll give you the low down," said Tony as we left the warehouse.

"Oh, shouldn't you introduce me to the warehouse keeper and the guys?" I asked Tony.

"Sure. Guys, this is Officer Erin Thorne. She is my replacement," said Tony in a loud voice.

Together we briskly strode to a couple of what looked like golf carts a little way from the main warehouse.

"Okay, this will be your ride," said Tony as we stopped by a royal-blue golf cart with white top. It was a custom job since it had four seats and a short bed at the rear.

I slid into the passenger side of the open vehicle. I let Tony drive.

"This facility is approximately three miles wide by three miles long. So it isn't very big, but when you're in a hurry or have to carry something heavy, this should do the trick."

"Tony, when are you going to leave our fair little town?" asked a heavy man wearing a straw western hat and a blue plaid shirt. He had just pulled up by the door of the warehouse in another cart, only his was candy-apple red. He turned and looked at us.

"As soon as I can, Mitch, as soon as I can," Tony answered as he pushed a button and turned on our cart. We started backing up and heard an explosion behind us.

Startled, I took a deep breath, then look toward the sound; but I knew it was Mitch.

"That was Mitch, wasn't it?" asked Tony. Without looking at the smoking cart, he slapped our cart into park, slid out, and ran toward Mitch.

"Yes, it was," I said as I jumped out of the cart and rushed to Mitch, too.

I had a head start, but soon I was just looking at Tony's back. Man, could he run.

We arrived at the side of the smoking cart. I crouched down and waited as Tony felt Mitch's neck for a pulse. I saw Tony smile and shake his head.

"Okay, Mitch, hang in there. The boys will be here in a minute."

The sound of a siren split the air and soon another motorized cart appeared, only this one had an enclosed back and there was an International Red Cross symbol on the side.

Two guys dressed in light green surgical scrubs jumped out and ran toward us.

"He's got a pulse, it's steady. Amazing, but you know what they say about mean men. Anyway, George, Bill, this is your scene. If I don't see you before I leave, take care," said Tony to the men as he stood up.

I stood up, too, and stepped back.

Tony took a step forward and introduced me. "Oh, guys, this is Erin Thorn. Erin, the blond one is George, and the dark guy is Bill. Guys, be nice."

I shook my head, laughing as we walked away. Tony had a smile on his face.

"Okay, and now for the rest of the tour," I said.

"Oh, yeah, back to my script. We have six buildings in our dome, or town, and the Elliot Space Station. We have one ship a day. The ship lands in the morning, the flight you were on, and it leaves in the late afternoon, the flight that I will be on," he said as he slid into the cart.

Rita Schulz

I slid into the cart next to him and he backed up, and then started forward.

"You just saw our warehouse. It's broken into two parts: international goods waiting for clearance, and domestic goods. The domestic goods are further split into two sections: goods awaiting exportation, and goods that have cleared and are waiting to be delivered. The entire facility is geared around mining and the support of that mining operation. Simple. Questions?" he asked.

I shook my head. So far so good.

"There are six buildings in our *town*—we use the term very loosely since there are only about one hundred and twenty people living here all together. There are about twenty who work at the Station itself, forty in the Warehouse and sixty miners. The biggest of the six buildings is the Warehouse that you were kissing the floor of a few minutes ago. Then there's a large, long building called the Store. That's over there. It's the one painted forest green. It contains a coffee shop, restaurant, grocery store, post office, movie theater, clothing store, bookstore...you get the drift. Then you have four dry mud colored barracks, where everyone lives."

13

"Stop. That's not what the brochure said. The brochure said this was a growing and lively town with all the features of a large city. Then it described what you just listed, but no one said it was all in one building," I said.

I was horrified. *This can't be true.* Then I remember Tony saying something about nine square miles. I'd thought he was joking or talking about the warehouse area, not the entire town.

There was no way on earth, or the moon, that I could live in something this tiny. There had to be more. Tony was again pulling my leg. He had to be. I could feel my heart start to beat harder. I looked around for a way out of this place. My mouth felt dry and my throat started to tighten.

"Of course that's what the brochure said. I wrote it. I've been here for fifteen years. The only way I can get off this rock is to have someone else come here and take this job. And you have, so I'm leaving," said Tony with a very smug smile on his face.

"What? No, absolutely not. I suffer from claustrophobia. I need to get out for a drive and to stretch my legs at least every second day if not every day. They lied to me! Therefore, the contract is void. It wasn't valid."

We heard what sounded like a police siren. I looked down the road to see another cart, a black-and-white police logo painted on its side. I hoped the police were going to check up on what happened to Mitch.

"Is it always so lively here?"

"Actually, it's a slow day. There wasn't much cargo on the flight that you were on."

"Okay, now tell me, when are you really leaving? This afternoon? Why?"

He laughed as he glanced at me. "For pretty much the reasons that you don't want to stay here. The walls are closing in on me. I've been stuck on this rock for fifteen years. I've taken online courses and gotten degrees in accounting and law. I've gotten pretty good at online poker too. By the way, the same restriction applies to you—the only way you can leave is to find a replacement, and that may take a while," he said and nodded to himself, gazing straight ahead.

We passed a second warehouse; the 'Store' and I saw that it had different entrances and doors with names of different services.

I realized that I was indeed in a mess. What I had told Tony was the truth: I had a very bad case of cabin fever. I wasn't great in enclosed spaces.

If I didn't get out of here, I would go downhill quickly. I could already feel my heart starting to pound and my hands getting damp with perspiration at the very thought that I was trapped. I noticed my breath was coming faster and faster.

"I'll figure out a way to get off this rock." I tried to take in deep, slow breaths, focusing on something else and not thinking that I was trapped in the small enclosure and would be for years and years and years. I felt like screaming.

"Up ahead is the barracks, as we fondly call them," Tony said in a flat voice.

I forced myself to listen to what he was saying. "Barracks? I thought I would have luxurious, state of the art accommodations with spectacular scenery?"

"Yeah, me again. Maybe I can get a job writing ad copy. What do you think?" asked Tony.

I nodded. "I can control this. I can control this," I said to myself in a low voice. I was determined not to let my anxiety start a panic attack. That was something I'd never had and never wanted to experience. But I knew I had to get out of this place. I didn't care what I had to do. I was going to get out.

Tony stopped the cart in front of the barracks. I looked him. He met my eyes and he nodded. "You've really got it bad, don't you?"

I shook my head. I didn't want a stranger to see me like this. My eyes were dry and burning. I blinked, trying to get some relief. I even tried smiling. I stepped out of the cart. My legs were shaking but I forced myself to move and followed Tony into the long, low, mud-colored barracks set on a dusty, rock-and-sand-strewn field.

Oh man, the quarters were ugly and depressing. It would be merciful to blow it up and start again.

"Do you get involved with crimes, like what happened to Mitch?" I hoped at least my work would be interesting. But I knew that in a very short while I wouldn't be able to concentrate on anything except finding a way out. I sensed any attempt to do so could get very dangerous.

There was an explosion somewhere in the distance. It sounded similar to the one that injured Mitch.

"Come on, I'm just picking up some things and then I'll be checking out. The shuttle leaves in a couple of hours," said Tony as he opened the barracks front glass door.

We walked down a long, dim corridor with wooden doors and brass number plates. We stopped in front of one of the doors and Tony opened it with an old-fashioned brass key.

"Tony, I'm sorry, but I can't stay here. I was hired under false pretenses. The company lied to me. Really, I can't stay here. Besides, I haven't even signed anything yet, except the document that you had me sign. Was that…" I stopped and looked at him.

Did he just screw me into being stuck here forever? I could feel myself getting angry. How could he have done that to me?

"No Erin. What you need to sign is a contract with either Elliot Space Station or the International Border and Immigration Service, they are the ones that would hire you or let you go with a contract."

"I haven't done that and I don't have a contract. Does that help? I have to go back to Earth. Please." I hated the pleading tone in my voice. I'd rather be shooting, blowing things up, or chasing after bad guys. This was not like me at all.

"Yeah, you're not the only one," he said as he opened the door and we walked into his cramped, beige, one-room studio.

I looked at him. "Please. What do I need to do to get out of here?"

He sat down on the one plastic chair in the room and motioned that I should sit on the twin bed in the corner. I did.

"Do you have three million dollars?"

"Don't be stupid. If I had three million dollars, I wouldn't be trying to get a job." I shook my head, trying to figure what Tony was talking about.

"The three million is a one-way flight from the moon to Earth."

"But I don't have three million dollars. So it really is a nonstarter." I was trying to be logical. I really didn't want to lie, cheat, or steal, but it seemed the company that hired me started it first. They lied. This may be the exception to my rule.

I heard another explosion. This blast, though small, was closer, maybe at the Store.

Tony seemed unfazed by the explosion. "That's fine. What kind of credit card do you have?"

"Why are there so many explosions? Tony, what is happening here?" I asked. I was getting a really horrible feeling that there was a major point missing.

"Never mind. I have Diamond Platinum; it will cover anything anywhere. I'll zip your ticket on my card, and when we get to Earth, I'll send the bill to Elliot Space Station. They'll have to cover it. And then I'll cancel my card. Good thing you haven't unpacked," said Tony, trying to smile.

He selected clothing from his closet and chest and put them next to me on the bed.

He started folding them, putting them in a dark brown, leather duffel bag.

"Actually, I forgot to pick up my luggage at the space station."

Another blast, shaking the walls, showered us in fine dust. It seemed to be right outside the front door.

"What's happening here? Why do I get the feeling that we're all prisoners? That once you come here, you can never, ever leave? They don't pay you enough for a trip home and they don't hire people except on a need-to basis. You are stuck here forever, aren't you?"

Tony looked at me and nodded. "We have to go now. We'll drive to the spaceport. We can pick up your things"

"Tony, please tell me, what's with the explosions?"

"It's the workers. They've had enough of the treatment, the lies and everything. They were shanghaied just as you were. It's happening. It's an all-out revolt. I was hoping the uprising would hold off for another couple of months, but since they attacked Mitch today with the small bomb, it's started. They won't do any damage to the dome, just all the buildings *in* the dome."

I looked out the window. Another blast went off. This one was at the far corner of the barracks. It seemed they were destroying the buildings, as Tony said, one by one.

"Come on. We have to go, now," said Tony as he grabbed the duffel bag and swung it over his shoulder, along with a black leather briefcase.

I followed him down the hall and to the cart.

It didn't take long to get to the warehouse. Once we got there, I saw that chunks of the walls and sections of the roof had disappeared. Tony showed me where the tunnels were for the goods and passengers. We drove our cart all the way into the circular holding area and got off. I collected my luggage and everything went as planned.

We met with no resistance or even questions at the ticket office. The crew behind the counter was nervous and kept looking at each other. They just handed us our tickets and didn't even check my documents.

I went to the ladies' room and changed from my uniform; by the time I got out, the crew had all left.

Then I heard explosions again. Only this time they sounded different. Bigger. It sounded like they were being set off outside the dome.

I met Tony. "The bombs are getting closer. You don't think..." I started to ask, but stopped as he slowly shook his head.

"Come on, let's go," he said. "We're going to have to move as quickly as we can, right to the ship."

That's when I felt the cement pad that we were standing on rock. Some of the walls were starting to buckle and pictures were falling off the walls.

I looked at Tony. I couldn't believe it. Maybe getting stuck in a small town under a dome wasn't so bad after all. No, I knew I couldn't do it. Leaving was the only option.

"Follow me," said Tony as he lengthened his stride. I walked quickly next to him. I saw the signs to the gate we would use to depart.

There was an explosion, right behind us as we passed the security station. I turned and saw there was a hole in the inner wall of the Station building. People were screaming and the roof started to come down in chunks around us.

Tony looked at me, grabbed my case, and started to run. I put my purse over my shoulder and ran right next to him.

The intercom came on. "All passengers with tickets for the flight this afternoon at four o'clock go directly to the departure lounge.

"The ship will be departing early, within the next fifteen minutes. Please make your way directly to the departure lounge!"

The floor shook again, twice more. We ran faster. People were falling all around us, screaming. Some because of the explosions, but most were knocked down by other people.

We had to go over, around, or through the entangled bodies.

I lost my balance and was knocked to my knees but picked myself up and continued to run.

I was starting to run slower, breathing hard and gasping for air by the time we got to the walkway to the ship.

The announcer was urging all passengers to board as we reached the waiting lounge. The gate staff stood by the door and didn't look at our tickets, they just waved us through as quickly as possible. Their ashen faces and flitting eyes told me the situation was growing more desperate by the moment.

I grabbed two seats together by the window and Tony swung into the seat next to me.

I had just belted in when the captain announced the hatch was closing and to prepare for liftoff.

Rebellion

Looking around, I saw there were still a few empty seats, but the crew was closing the hatch. There were no safety announcements on this flight.

I could hear the warning blasts from the ship, signaling immediate departure. I looked at Tony and silently thanked him.

The ship started to rumble and shake as the engines warmed up. Soon I heard the metallic sound as the gantries holding the ship in place moved away. Now was a critical point and closed my eyes. The ship would make it into orbit or it would be destroyed taking us with it.

Suddenly a burst of thrust from the rockets slammed me back in my seat. The rumble of the engines increased. Ignition. The pressure increased as I felt the surge of take off from the moon's surface. My mouth tasted dry and metallic, my breathing rapid in my ears. Tony had gripped my hand and was squeezing it tightly.

I held my breath and closed my eyes for a few seconds.

There were no more announcements from the captain as I was pressed into the seat by an increase in gravity as the ship accelerated to escape velocity.

I relaxed as my heart rate slowed. We had left the gray surface of the moon behind.

I'd made it. I had managed to live through a rebellion on the moon.

We were returning to Earth.

PARTY CENTRAL

RAMONA SMILED TO HERSELF.

She was going to retire in eight more days. And two days after she retired she and her husband Wayne were moving to her dream home on a quiet island off the coast of British Columbia. Everything was going exactly as she had planed.

She was of medium height with shoulder length brown hair, gray eyes, and a generous mouth. Her features were pleasing although a bit ordinary, but when she smiled her face lit up and her enthusiasm shone through her eyes.

Ramona stood by the white front door closet and heard a soft meow. There was a soft bump of a small body next to her leg. She looked down to see, Susie her little chocolate Siamese cat.

She quickly bent down and gave Susie a quick pat on her pillowy soft fur.

Ramona gabbed her dark-blue wool jacket, her black leather shoulder bag, and the book she was currently reading, and quietly left the small neat townhouse.

She could smell the tall fir trees that grew in the roundabout at the center of their driveway circle. It was such a strong refreshing scent she could almost taste it, and tangy scent always put a smile on her face.

She walked the few steps to where her car was parked in its spot directly in front of her home. She paused to look at the rusted out car parked almost right on her bumper of her car.

She took in a deep breath and tapped the side of her bag with her natural rounded fingernail as she decided what to do.

Their neighbor, Max had parked right behind her again leaving a huge gap behind him, and now she couldn't get out.

Ramona really detested waking up her neighbors because it was always their young son who answered the door in the mornings while the parents slept in. But she had to get to work.

It didn't seem to matter how many fines they received, Max and his wife still didn't follow the rules.

Although this was one thing Ramona wasn't going to miss. All the rules in this townhouse complex, and everyone watching everything you do.

She was looking forward to the large piece of property she and Wayne had bought on Goat Island. It was a small island just outside of Vancouver between the Mainland and Vancouver Island. They would finally have the freedom and the quiet they both craved after living and working in Vancouver all their lives.

It was a mild morning for the middle of February. At six forty-five the sun had risen and the increasing breeze was refreshing.

The trees stirred and Ramona heard bird song. She hummed to herself as she walked up to the neighbors white front door that was identical to hers, except for the number. The only difference between their units was the neighbor's door looked pitted, scared, and old. She and Wayne had always been careful to take good care of their property.

Ramona knocked on the dented, scratched white door and sighed as she waited for it to open.

She didn't want a confrontation, especially today since she had been in such a good mood. She was happy.

She started to hum to herself again when suddenly the door opened with a bang.

The smell of stale smoke and stale beer wafted over her. As it entered her mouth she closed her lips to keep from coughing. Her stomach rolled and she almost gagged, but she swallowed and managed to stop herself from losing her morning cereal.

Before stood an awful sight.

Her neighbor Max in all his glory, unshaven, unkempt, with his hairy potbelly hanging over his grey striped boxers scratching his ass looking down at her. She shuddered as she looked up and kept her eyes fixed on his blood shot ones to avoid looking at the rest of the man.

"Yeah, what do you want?" Max asked as he belched in her face.

"Your car. Could you move it please?" asked Ramon keeping her voice level and trying not to breath to deeply.

She had to focus on the remaining eight days after which she would leave this place with its looky-loos and it's Maxes. That was her goal. Her pot of gold at the end of the rainbow.

29

Max shook his head grabbed his car keys off a hook by the door, belched again, and walked out in his stocking feet. He opened the door of his rusty, green sixty- four Mustang got in. The old car rumbled to life and he backed up.

Without waiting to thank him, Ramona quickly got into her little red Sunfire and drove to work. Thankfully they lived close to the office so she made it for her seven-thirty start time.

She started to shred her soon to be obsolete paperwork first thing in the morning. Her copies of old files and information she had collected from the various jobs that she'd had in the organization. Years of training, information, and work she had done soon were all gone.

She hummed to herself as she started feeding paper into the machine and watched as little strips of paper came out to fall into the bin.

The air was kept cool in the computer printer room where the shredder was and soon Ramona was shivering in her light blouse and slacks.

Ramona went back to her small, cramped cubical to get her sweater. She gazed at her plants. She had brought in her own variegated ivy and spider plants.

She'd read somewhere they helped produce oxygen and were helpful in an indoor environment. At first they had done poorly, but she brought in a full spectrum lamp and soon she and the plants seemed to feel better.

Once she finished the shredding for the day she packed up her light and her plants in the box she had emptied and then took them down to the car park.

She checked her schedule and realized that she had a coffee date with one of her friends, and then another buddy was taking her out to lunch.

She enjoyed some of the attention and she knew that she would miss her friends. Ramona felt her throat tighten and the thought off not seeing her friends again. But they were building a large enough house so that her friends could come visit them on their peaceful island. Many of them had said that they would. In fact she had already booked a few of her friends to come over in the summer time. She was looking forward to that.

***

Ramona pulled up in front of her town home and stopped short as she saw a children's bicycle behind the bush next to her parking spot. She shook her head.

Party Central

She parked the car leaving the engine running she popped out and moved her neighbor's child's bike then parked in her designated space.

Ramona knew that she would miss some of the people, but the traffic, the crowds and the noise, that they could keep.

Although she and Wayne did enjoy hosting and going to parties she was sure that they could get all that on their little island too. They weren't the only people there after all.

Ramona parked her car and went into her home ready to tackle another room.

Tonight they were going to clean out the basement and do a real purge on all of their books. She and Wayne were both avid readers and had collected quite a few pocket books. The majority of them had to go. If they were in very good shape they would sell them, and the remainder they would be donate to the local literacy program.

Susie met her at the front door. She quickly gave her a pat and went upstairs to get changed into a pair of soft comfortable faded jeans and tee shirt. She then she went back downstairs to take a quick look at how many empty boxes they had in the basement.

The basement had the smell of old paper books and comfortable leather chairs.

"Ramona, I'm home," she heard Wayne call from the main floor above.

"I'm downstairs. We're going to need more boxes."

Ramona climbed the stairs to the main level to give Wayne a quick hug. "Do you want to go and get them or should I?"

"Why don't you get them and on the way home stop off at the chicken place and bring home some dinner. I'll start packing up."

Wayne leaned down and kissed Ramona on her lips. Then he rubbed his chin, with its five o'clock stubble against her soft cheek. She laughed and pushed him away.

Wayne was a man about six feet tall and on the slender side. His hair was beginning to recede but he was still handsome as ever. He was retiring the same day as Ramona, although he didn't seem as excited as she did.

"Eight more sleeps." She gave him another quick hug.

"Yes, dear. We can go over this weekend and take some stuff for the house. I dropped by the builder's office on the way from home and picked up the key. He says it's ready."

Wayne held out the bright new brass key to her as he picked up Susie who was waiting for her greeting.

"Great, all the utilities kick in starting tomorrow. We'll have heat, and light everything we need in our new house." Ramona was getting excited.

Susie started to purr loudly as Wayne bent down to pet her soft sleek fur and scratch her just below her ear something the cat loved.

"I can hardly wait to see it. We haven't been there since before December and only the foundation was in then. What if —"

"I'm sure that everything is fine. The sub-contractor will meet us at the site. Or should I say our new home." Wayne held up the keys jangling them in front of Ramona.

She laughed as she pulled on her jacket and picked up her purse. She knew that everything would be fine with their new home. They had had a few glitches along the way, but everything was fine now.

They had rented a van and would take some of their goods over now. Ramona knew exactly what they would need and had already packed the pre-move items.

On the weekend they would take over most of their kitchen.

She was also taking along a set of sheets and a new quilt set so that when the bed was moved in she could quickly make it up. It would give them a nice clean bed to sleep in on their first night in their new home.

Ramona had mapped and measured out where everything was going to go. She had even decided where her plants were going to go, and had gotten special stands for her rabbits-foot fern and her purple and hot pink bougainvillea.

Not to be out done the variegated fichus she had taken cuttings from and propagated at work two years ago and planted them in a pot to take with her. It was now a nice sized little tree, and had a lovely small teak table to call home.

With the southern exposure they would do well in the living room with it's cream-colored walls, soft white sheer drapes, and red oak plank hardwood floor. Her special plants would be going with them in this first trip too while others would come later with the furniture.

It would be a full day. They had reservations and would go over on the first ferry and home on the last.

It was a grey day and sprinkled on the way to the ferry and on the way across to their island.

Party Central

***

Standing on the ferry deck she drank in the smell of the salt water and her ears were filled the cries of the gray and while gulls that rode the breeze over the ferry searching for cast off food.

For the first time in along time she felt her shoulders relax as the stress of her job and the city was released from within her.

As they arrived at their new home it started to pour with rain.

Ramona was doing her best to sit still. She was a bundle of nervous excitement and clenched and unclenched her hands as they pulled up the driveway.

The house was just as she had imagined it. The view was breathtaking. Their property overlooked the ocean and the islands beyond receding toward Vancouver. The emerald green islands looked like stepping stones against the sky blue water.

And the best thing was that where they were situated so that no one could build in front of them to obstruct the view.

They managed to keep most of the tall fir, cedar, and arbutus trees on their property as well as the native ferns and salal. With the rain it brought out all their natural scents. The air was thick with the scent and sounds of rain and forest.

All of her dreams and plans over the last ten years were about to be fulfilled.

They both opened the car door and like two children on Christmas morning ran toward the house. They stopped to stand under the overhang out of the pelting rain over the front porch of their new home and grinned at each other.

Wayne opened the front door and looked at Ramona. He knew how much this meant to her and how hard she hard worked toward this. "Do you want me to carry you over the threshold?"

She laughed and shook her head. She then took his strong hand in hers wanting them both to share in the moment. Together they walked through the wide double doors into the foyer.

It was exactly as she had planned. It was beautiful.

The odor of fresh paint and wood surrounded them. She slowly drank it all in. It was perfect.

From the copper colored tile entry to the grey granite counters in the kitchen and in the bathrooms. The master bedroom, painted a dark cream with white trim, had a two-person soaker tub with a large privacy window so that you could look out at the incredible view while you took a bubble or Jacuzzi bath, and the shower was large enough to have four people in it.

It even had a built in seat.

Wayne went to the attached double car garage, opened it, and drove the van in. He brought Susie out her carrier. The cat could wander around the new house and start getting used to the new place.

Soon he and Ramona had everything unloaded from the van.

"Well, honey we're doing really well unloading. Do you want to go out for a bite of lunch?" asked Wayne as he put away the last glass in the kitchen cupboard.

"What's that noise?" said Ramona as she came from the master bedroom with a bunch of wooden clothes hangers in her hands.

There was a large crash in that came from the living room followed by a loud song with a distinctive Reggae beat.

Ramona looked at Wayne, a quizzical look on her face as if he had the answer to the noise. He just shrugged his shoulders and shook his head.

They followed the noise and discovered in the middle of their beautiful tranquil living room were and assortment of cats and rats and elephants all about three feet high in a long conga line.

The tiny animals were all up on their hind legs wearing either colorful long

Hawaiian shirts or pants. On their heads they wore white party hats with bright colorful pink and purple pom-poms on top, and green boas adorned their shoulders.

Susie was walking between them and rubbing against their legs.

"What are you and what are you doing in my house!" yelled Ramona.

They had destroyed her plants and her curtains. Now they were doing a good job in gouging up the hardwood floors.

She quickly ran to the laundry room and grabbed a broom. She raced into the living room and turned off the music after opening the front doors.

Wayne picked up Susie who had come into the kitchen purring loudly. He put her into the furnace room and closed the door.

"Get out. Get out my house of my house. Get out now!" Ramona yelled at the top of her voice as she chased the strange things out of the house using the broom alternately as a club or a baseball bat.

They kept on dancing and shouting, "Party! Party!" as they walked past her in a long conga line.

Her ears rang with the noise they made leaving which almost her deafened her.

She went into the kitchen and looked at Wayne who had gone back to the kitchen to finish putting the coffee cups away.

"Wayne, did you see that?" she said not trusting herself.

"See what? I heard a lot of loud music, but I thought it was just an alarm clock radio that went off." He went and let Susie out of the furnace room.

"No. We just had a bunch of three foot high cats and rats and elephants dancing in our living room," she said.

Wayne looked at her and nodded, but didn't say anything.

She stopped and went into the living room to see if there was any evidence of what she had seen.

Ramona doubted herself. She must have imagined it.

It must be stress.

She took a deep breath to steady herself and opened her eyes. No the mess in her living room was still there.

She could feel herself start to shake and knew that if she let go it would be a long time before she could control herself again.

This is crazy. Or I'm going crazy.

"Honey, its just stuff."

Wayne had come into the living room to stand by her shoulder. "It can always be fixed."

Just then the front doors opened up and the conga line came back into the house and into the living room. Susie joined them.

Ramona went into the kitchen and dragged Wayne back so he could see for himself. The living room had been destroyed. The curtains were torn down, plants destroyed, and the floor was ruined.

Ramona looked at Wayne for an answer and then started to cry. She stopped and wiped her eyes with the back of her hand. No way was she going to let these creatures ruin her perfect plan. She'd get them out of the one way or another.

An exterminator. That's what we need.

Ramona quickly picked up the phone and dialed directory assistance. "I need the number of an exterminator."

"That might not be a good idea, Ramona," said Wayne.

Ignoring him she jotted down the number the operator gave d dialed. The phone rang once and a man answered.

"Hi, this is Ramona Fielder at 888 Sunwood Drive. I need an exterminator."

Ramona looked at Wayne who had joined her and smiled at him confident that the problem would go way and then they would clean the house. They could still save their dream.

"What exactly is the problem, ma'am?" came a deep voice over the telephone.

Suddenly, Ramona realized how foolish she would sound asking an exterminator to get rid of the three-foot high cats and rats and elephants from her house. She hung up the phone. She couldn't have the people living on her island thinking she was a loony.

Suddenly the music was on again. She looked hopelessly as the conga line wound its way past them. The last one in line passed her. It was a cute Siamese cat who looked exactly like their Susie, except it was three feet tall.

Wayne reached out to grasp one of the cat's legs and gently pulled her out of the line.

"Who are you and what's going on here?" he asked the cat.

"We're from all over the galaxy. This is one of the Party Planets. We come here for our holidays." The cat-like thing stood in front of them with her arms and feet still moving to the beat of the music.

Aliens? Party planets? My new house?
"Wayne, do something."

Tears streamed down Ramona's cheeks.

"How come we've never seen or heard of you before?"

"The gateway into your house just opened up again. Mars was in the way until recently. But now we can come and party. Your Susie sure is cute and really nice. She says your really great people and like to party. Want to join us?" Then the cat-like alien ran after the line and quickly joined them again.

The dancers came around again and this time they had the pots and pans out of the cupboards and were banging on them to the beat of the music.

Wayne took Ramona by the hand and led her to the van, opened her door, and made sure t she was belted in the passenger side.

"Lets go for lunch. When we come back we'll see then how everything is. Okay?"

Wayne was right. They needed a break for this madness. What else were they to do? This couldn't be real and it would give them time to think.

Ramona looked at him and slowly nodded her head letting him take the lead. She wasn't hungry but time alone with him would do her good.

After a quick light lunch at a local dinner they came back to their new home.

They parked in the garage Wayne had forgotten to close, but Ramona didn't say anything.

They went into the kitchen and were met by a purring Susie. Everything thing looked normal and not the mess that had been there when they left.

Ramona and Wayne cautiously entered the living room. There were two grey humanoid like beings dressed plain gray work overalls. One was tall while the other was shorter. They were working, cleaning up the mess made by the conga line.

And everything was almost back to normal. One of the aliens was sweeping the floor with a straw broom while the other was putting the final touches on the plants.

The curtains were hung and the floor looked as if no one had ever walked on before. The house even smelled like no one had ever been there before, all fresh and clean.

The taller alien with the broom spoke as he kept on sweeping.

"Sorry for the mess, but we cleaned it all up. Just out of curiosity, why did you build a home right in the middle of a Travel Gate? You must really like to party."

"How often does this happen?" asked Wayne.

"We come through this destination about once a month," he answered as he stopped sweeping. He pulled out a sheet of paper from his pocket and looked at it. "Yeah, every four weeks on Saturday at 12:00. And we're punctual," he said with obvious pride.

Every week? Oh, no. My peace and quiet.

***

Wayne and Ramona pulled up at their townhouse late that afternoon after a very quiet trip home. Neither of them had said a word to each other. They were each lost in their own thoughts.

Ramona went into their townhouse and sat down on a kitchen chair. She just stared ahead, not seeing anything.

Wayne let Suzie into the house and soon she was weaving between their legs and emitting soft encouraging meows.

Ramona looked down at her and started to say something, but stopped. What was there to say?

"Honey, we'll think of something," said Wayne trying to comfort her.

"What can we do? It must be something in the water or the air. It's not real, Wayne. What we saw wasn't real."

"Well ..."

"Oh come on, what you read and see on television isn't real. You do know that," said Ramona. She looked at Wayne as if trying to decide if he was just trying to humor her or he was being serious.

"Oh sure, Ramona I know it can't be real, but what if it is?"

"I say lets move in like we planned next week and see how it goes?"

Ramona slowly nodded.

That's all they could really do she thought as she could feel herself start to plan again. The alien said they come by once every four weeks on Saturday at 12:00. Now that gave her something to work with.

***

Ramona's last day and retirement party went as planned. The party was very nice, with good presents and speeches accompanied a few tears. Wayne had similar send off at his job.

The move had gone well too.

Ramona had postponed her friend's visits that summer. She told them they were going to have a second honeymoon, and would need a little more time to settle into their new routine.

The fourth Saturday came. The large polished brass kitchen wall clock showed 12:05.

There was no sign of the aliens. No music, no conga line, nothing. Ramona started to relax. They'd obviously imagined everything.

Ramona and Wayne sat in their large open kitchen having a late brunch of fresh bran muffins with fruit and finishing off an excellent cup of coffee.

She knew they were safe. She could feel the tension in her body starting to melt way like sun-warmed butter. It had all been their imagination.

"Yes. I know what your thinking and I agree. I don't know what came over us that day. All I can think of it must have been mass hallucination, well I guess mass is the wrong word, but you know what I mean." Wayne smiled at her.

She nodded at him. Their life was perfect. It was quiet and ordered. Susie sat with them in the kitchen waiting too.

She almost spewed a mouthful of coffee across the table when a sudden burst of noise from the living room erupted.

"Now arriving planet Earth. Hoop! Hoop! Party! Party! Party!" They heard yelling and shouting from the living room. Then they heard the blaring of music and they could feel the vibration of many feet stomping on the floor.

"No, it's not possible. It can't be real," cried Ramona as she felt her calmness, her serenity shatter.

They stood up, followed by Susie, and went into the living room. Sure enough there were the little aliens and the conga line winding it's way through their home.

"Well, Ramona what do you think?" Wayne reached out to take her hand in his as she shook her head.

"What are you talking about? This was supposed to be our quite life. You know read some books, go for long walks. Sit on the porch and watch the sunsets," she said as she sniffled.

"Yeah well, we could do that later. Why don't we do a little exploring first? I bet we could see some really interesting sites. And we could always come back to Party Central and sit on the porch when we're ready?

Ramona looked at Wayne, a confused look on her face, all her planning. Her world had totally changed. But was that necessarily bad? This could be the end of her nice orderly world. Was she ready to take a chance like this?

She looked into the eyes of her husband and realized that he had never really been completely sold of her dream of "retirement".

Oh, well. When you can't fight 'em join 'em.

Wayne was right. They could always come back and sit on the porch when they were ready.

The conga line came past them again only this time Wayne, Ramona, and Susie and joined it.

Party time!

ONCE UPON A TIME

"ONCE UPON A time, not that long ago, there was a city called Vancouver, in a province called British Columbia, in a country called Canada. This city had millions of people in it and huge buildings. The buildings were so tall the sunlight never reached the ground, everything was in shadow all day and all night."

I paused to gaze at my audience. Their mouths hung open and their eyes were round with disbelief.

My audience was three small children, one little boy, and two little girls, not one over the age of six. They started to push each other as they sat under an old blanket in front of the fire.

The others had finished their evening chores and settled in front of the fire as well. I hoped by the telling of stories and the singing of songs that some of the old information would be preserved for future generations.

"Jenna, go on," said one of the little girls as she shoved the little boy who was trying to get her attention by pulling her blonde braid.

"Yeah, Jenna, go on. By the way, what's a million?" asked my husband Grant in his deep bass voice.

I glanced at him and gave him a smile. He had a way of always making me feel good. I continued my story.

"Do you see the rocks on the hill, and the gravel we climbed to look for the salmon?" I asked the children.

The children nodded at me and smiled. I had their attention again. "Well, there are probably a million rocks there. Do you see the large skeletons of the old redwoods and cedars?" They nodded. "Well, these buildings were even higher than some of them."

I heard the crackle and pop of the dead wood in our fire and smelled the dust and dirt a short distance from the cave we used as a shelter.

I swallowed, but my mouth was so dry that my tongue stuck to the roof of it. I licked my cracked lips anyway to give them a little moisture, but I was left with the metallic taste of blood.

I watched Grant give some water to one of the children and the other two asked for some, too. I looked at him and handed him my ration.

He nodded and smiled at me as he gave them a few swallows each. It wasn't much, but it would have to do.

He returned my water flask and I took a small sip, just enough to rinse my mouth, and slowly swallowed the remaining few drop. I quickly sealed up the flask to make sure that none of the precious liquid evaporated.

We sat in front of a cave in North Vancouver. There was once a temperate rain forest here but now it was as dry as a dessert. That was before "The Event", as we called it.

We were fortunate to be living in Vancouver. When the comet hit it was one-third of the way around the world, deep in the Atlantic Ocean. It wasn't the original hit: it was the aftermath that caused the worst damage. There were storms, fires, tsunamis and flooding. The entire planet felt as if it was pitched to one side and shaken, as if a terrier that had gotten hold of a rat and was trying to snap its neck. I was certain that this half of North America was going to break off at some fault line. The entire city was leveled.

Gone were the impressive tall building with their icy glass walls. Gone were the bridges, all fallen onto the ground or into the water they spanned. The highways and sky train were just partial twisted pathways going nowhere.

All that was left were stumps of a once thriving civilization.

A large percentage of the population had died as each new and more devastating catastrophe had washed the earth clean. Until there was only a couple of handfuls of people left. At least that's all that we had encountered so far.

But as suddenly as it had started it stopped.

Then it was quiet. Not a sound. No barking dogs, no birds, no cars, no radios. Nothing.

Silence was one of the hardest things to get used to. I had always had background noise around me: the sounds of cars or airplanes, the constant hum of electricity. The quiet was deafening. Luckily I had Grant and now we had the others. The sounds of their movements helped to ease the feeling that I was completely alone.

Gone were the tall majestic evergreens and the dense forest floor covered with fern and salal. Before, the forest had been a place where there was rich spongy soil underfoot and you heard the constant bubbling of ice-cold streams and the piney taste of cool forest air was thick on the tongue and face.

Now everything was dead and dry.

We needed water.

We found shelter when we traveled from South Hill in Vancouver to the caves and canyons of North Vancouver. But we would need a better shelter, a place with water and somewhere to rebuild.

We had been hit hard in the last three months, but it seemed the situation was stabilized. We hoped.

"Lucy, would you like some help with the children?" I asked as I finished the last of the song requests and put my guitar away.

Lucy was a pretty little Chinese woman who was at the end of her pregnancy. Her belly was large and distended.

"No, I'm fine. It's the least I can do with me like this right now."

There were only twelve adults we encountered as we traveled across Vancouver. We had called out as we went and the dogs had gotten good at scenting and finding people. That's how we had found Kent, a man in his mid- twenties, a banker and Winston, the little boy. They had both been trapped in rubble, but Grant and I managed to dig them out.

In total we had three women and myself. I was past childbearing age so I knew that I wasn't as important as the other women. I also looked at my husband Grant. We were traditionalist and our vows meant a lot to each other. But that was then and this was now.

Times had changed a lot of things, but our marriage? I sighed as the hard thoughts and ideas came to me.

In the end that seemed to have been what killed most of the population being killed where they lived or trapped in the buildings not able to get out. Then it was lack of electricity, medication and sanitation. It seemed that for a long time we had one epidemic after another and only the strong and the lucky lived through it.

"Everyone, I think that we need to talk. It's time to have a meeting. Let's say in about ten minutes?" said Grant.

I almost said that most of us didn't have watches since most people used to use their cell phones to check the time, but now there wasn't any electricity, the grid was completely down, and it wouldn't be up for a very long time, if ever. But old habits were hard to break sometimes.

Lucy came back from tucking the children into their beds at the back of the cave. It was cooler there and easier to protect them from the predators that had become more and more aggressive.

We had already had run-ins with bears and had a cougar sighting. There were packs of dogs that had quickly gone feral and were getting bolder. Luckily we found rifles and handguns in the local Gold and Gun store.

We had to teach each other how to shoot. "Okay, I'm here. Let's get the show on the road," said Lucy as she carefully lowered herself onto a fallen log that we had pulled over to the side of the fire pit.

I looked at everyone and waited. We had all been talking about what we needed to do to survive.

It was late spring and warm. I wasn't sure if the planet had shifted its axis and we were going to have warmer weather. For all I knew we had been pushed closer to the sun, but I really didn't think so. I wished I had paid more attention to some of those science and discovery programs when I had the chance to.

Before the comet hit we were told that it wasn't as big as the one that had caused the dinosaurs to become extinct. But I wondered how they really knew; after all they weren't here then. It was all a guess as far as I know. These were the same people who said we should make sure that we had enough food and water for about a week or two.

Boy, were their estimates off. Or perhaps they downplayed the Event so that people wouldn't panic. People did anyway. When cars plugged up the all of the exits out of the city, they tried walking and thousands of people were caught out in the open during the worst of it.

"Okay, we need to find water," Kent said as he started the conversation.

"We need a good supply of food. The kids need milk. We have enough powdered milk from the grocery stores to last for a while, but fresh is better," said Lucy.

"I've made up a list of things that we need. It's a long list and includes everything from horses, cows, and goats to bees and chickens and nuts and seeds. And tools, we need tools too," said Grant as he pulled out a piece of paper from his dirt crusted jeans pocket.

I nodded and smiled. It was going well. Grant and I had spoken earlier about some of the things that were important to have.

"Bees, what the hell are we going to do with bees?" asked Dorothy, a woman in her early thirties. She had long brown hair the she was now wearing in a long braid. A hairstyle that most of the woman had adopted these days, myself included.

"A lot of things: They naturally will help pollinate the crops for us and will produce honey, probably our only sugar, as well as wax that we can use to make candles," said Grant.

Listening to him made me proud. He had actually listened to me when we had discussed things that I had been thinking about even before the Event.

I watched the other women, and Kent the other male. I knew that if we were the only people that were left in this area we would need to make all the babies we could. We didn't know how the rest of the world fared, there could be pockets where others had survived, but so far it didn't look great for the human race. And the only way to improve the odds of human survival would be to have the most diverse genetic pool that we could. It was long range planning, but we had to take everything into account.

I felt bile rise up in my throat. I loved my husband, but we were in our fifties. I couldn't help by having children but he still could. I knew that he took the vows we made to each other seriously, but these were different times.

"Who knows anything about stupid bees?" asked Shirley, a teenage girl from a comfortable gated community.

"I do," I answered.

"It's not the only thing we need. But Jenna and I know a man from our old neighborhood that has the knowledge that we need. He has the farmer and woodsman stuff down pat. He even built his own bread kiln in his back yard. He heated it with wood and it worked perfectly. He grew all his own vegetables and even had a beehive.

The food was fresh and delicious. This was all in the city."

I waited for them to reach the only conclusion that they could. I watched as each face reached it.

"Someone is going to have to go into the middle of the city and see what can be saved. There may be other things we can salvage in time, but I know where he lives and where the bees.

He was alive when we left, but he wanted to stay there waiting for his children hoping that they would come home."

I smoothed down my top as I stood and wrapped my shawl tightly around me. My fingers played with the short fringe at the ends and I knew that I was showing my nervousness. The dogs at my feet stood up and stretched. They looked at me waiting.

"I volunteer to go to South Hill and see what I can come back with. I'll copy the list we have and if there is anything else that we need, that we can't get close by, we'll add it to the list," I said.

I was pleased with myself; my voice was calm and steady even though the acid in my belly was tearing me apart. I looked around the dying fire and looked at everyone in turn and smiled confidently but I hadn't looked at Grant once.

I had already spoken and discussed this with Grant and Ken and they had both agreed. Neither had been happy with the idea and Grant and I had discussed it until there weren't any more words. All we could do is love each other while we had the time to be together.

"We need you here to help us. And you can't go by yourself it's too dangerous," said Lucy looking afraid.

I looked her in the eyes and lied. "Thanks, Lucy. That's sweet of you; it's not that bad. I'll be fine. I won't be gone that long and I bet that I'll be back before that baby of your comes. Okay?"

The odds of me making it back weren't very good. We had had a really difficult time getting here in the first place.

A couple of the other females looked at each other and at Lucy. The two of us were the only women experienced in having children and they were counting on us. But they only needed one, so I was the one that should go. That might make things easier for Grant and the other women.

I kept telling myself I was being logical and making a hard decision for the best interest of the group.

"I'll be leaving as soon as possible. I'll be walking, but I would like to take Buster along with me."

Buster was a large golden retriever and would be good company on the trip.

If I was lucky and got some things that were awkward to carry, I was planning to hitch a drag carrier to him.

"You can keep Page." I said to Grant. "She's good at finding and catching rabbits so you'll have some fresh meat for the pot while I'm gone. And most importantly I can be on the lookout for water as I travel. I'll make a map and keep a journal about what I find. That way we can use the information when I get back to decide if we should go and where we should go to."

I knew I had them. I had erased any doubts about leaving our little happy group at the mention of water.

I didn't want to go, but I was the best choice, actually the only choice. I had the best chance of getting there and getting back as quickly as possible while the others took care of the hunting and fishing and protecting the camp.

I watched them as they all started to nod in agreement. We had up to now always stuck together and helped each other this was the first time our little group was splitting up and no one liked it. But we needed the information and the bees, it had to be done and they all realized it.

**

I made good time getting out of North Vancouver.

While the roads were buckled and the buildings pretty much leveled it wasn't too bad. I was getting used to it and finding ways around the worst of the destruction. It was still going to be a long journey, probably a good week.

I was lucky and soon found little ponds of ground water to keep Buster and me from becoming dehydrated. I stopped at grocery store that was not one of the ones we were using for supplies and got enough supplies for the journey.

It really was incredible how everything in the city was so much cleaner than it ever was before the Event. The air was so clear that it was almost painful to look at the horizon. You used to see just a faint outline of the Gulf Islands, but now you could see the shorelines and each island standing out from the others.

At night the sky was so clear and the moon and stars so close that you could almost touch them. The light from the stars high overhead, hung in the air like diamonds scattered on a dark blue velvet curtain. And the moon was a large pale white pearl hanging there, shining gently down on the new world. It all looked so normal, but the stars weren't really in the place that they should be, or that I remembered that they should be. The Big Dipper was there, but it was low in the horizon.

I couldn't remember if it was that way or if it should be directly overhead. We really needed books from the library another thing that we would have to do soon.

On the third day of going up Indian Arm, Buster and I found a boat that was still seaworthy and we took it across and entered Vancouver. When we landed and I pulled the boat ashore for the return trip. Buster jumped out of the boat and ran around, he stopped, stood still and lifted his muzzle into the air. He moved his head back and forth as he tested the air to locate the scent that had caught his attention.

I heard a deep guttural woof and a heavy shuffling lumbering sound that didn't belong to any dog I had ever encountered.

It was a bear; I quickly dropped my pack and got my rifle out. It was a light rifle and knew that it wouldn't do much good in this situation.

"Buster, come here. Stay," I said to the dog in a firm tone.

I knew that the best plan was to get out of the area as soon as possible. I didn't know if it was a sow with cubs or a big old male bear. I knew that their normal food wouldn't be available this year and that would be making them hungry and mean.

I picked up my pack and slung it onto my back as I tried to grab Buster. But Buster saw the bear and started barking; the bear came around the corner of a low wrecked building and charged straight at us. It was a big male and it was mad. I looked around for the nearest building that would give us shelter. It was across a wide expanse of road and rock. I knew we wouldn't make it, but had to try.

I steadied the rifle and quickly fired off two shots and yelled and screamed as loud as I could as I ran toward the bear waving my arms. Then I stopped and ran the other way still screaming and waving my arms over head.

My idea of shock and awe didn't work and the bear didn't turn away. Instead he stood up on his hind legs and roared and he swiped his lethal front paws at us.

"Come on, Buster, run!" I yelled at him as I led the way across the road.

He didn't follow me.

I heard a combination of roaring from the bear and frenzied barking and growling from Buster.

I glanced over my shoulder as I ran. Buster was playing a dangerous game with the bear. He ducked between the bear's paws, snapped his teeth and then ran away. He managed it a few times and then I heard a loud horrible yelping and a howl of pain.

I got to the building, stopped and turned to look at Buster and raised my rifle. I couldn't shoot; the bear had him against his chest between his front paws. Then I saw it drop Buster, lift a paw and rake its claws down Buster. I watched him go limp, his head hanging to one side and I knew that he was dead.

The bear picked him up, shook Buster again, dropped him then turned and headed toward Burnaby.

Buster had saved me. Tears filled my eyes and I started to sob. I leaned against the building and swallowed hard trying to catch my breath. I couldn't believe that Buster was dead. It happened so quickly. He was a brave dog; a good dog and I would miss him. I started to cry again, and rubbed my eyes hard with my hand.

I was all alone.

I had no one to even talk too, but I couldn't stop. I knew that people were waiting for me and I had to press on. If this mission were to be successful I would have to keep going while there was daylight. I started walking again.

The following day, the fifth, I got to Knight Road and followed it all the way to South Hill and to my old home. It was so strange walking in the old neighborhood a place that was so familiar and now looked so different.

The worst was the smell. The sewage system must have broken and there was no one to take care of the bodies of the people and their pets.

I heard the yowl of feral cats and saw a small pack of midsized dogs, but they stayed away from me. I knew that I had to be very careful. Individually they were fine, but as a pack they could easily take down and kill a person.

I looked up and saw smoke coming from the back of old man Kurt's place and I smiled. My trip was not a waste. Now all I had to do was to convince him to come with me.

His knowledge and experience in the old ways of growing crops and taking care of animals could mean the difference between our survival and the extinction of the human race. I felt that with him we had a chance, a good chance.

I went around the side of the house and stepped over the fallen wooden fence that used to separate his property from his neighbor's. There was no one there anymore so it wasn't needed.

"Kurt, it's Jenna, your neighbor from across the street."

I waited. There was no sound, no answer.

"Kurt. Are you home?" I called again.

"Ya. Come on," said a weak trembling voice.

I heard the bark of a dog as I came around the corner of the ruined house. There was a tan shepherd looking warily at me. It's barking became frenzied. I froze.

"Kurt. You got yourself a dog?"

He had never had the time for dogs, preferring cats as company.

"Lucky. Enough," said Kurt.

The dog quieted and I moved forward.

I found Kurt. He was lying on a sleeping bag under a tarp that he had strung between four tall logs. It looked kind of like a teepee. He looked very old and grey. His eyes were sunken and bloodshot.

I was shocked and upset at the change in him, but I knew that I couldn't let it show. We really needed him.

"What happened, Kurt?" I asked as I knelt down beside him.

"Well, it's like I say. You never know, do you?"

I leaned over and felt his forehead. He didn't have a fever.

"No, it's my heart. No more medicine," he said.

"I'm waiting for the kids. They should be home soon," he mumbled to himself. "Everything's gone. They're all dead, you know."

"Kurt, I'm going to make you some tea from foxglove. Okay? We'll try it weak first."

"I don't have any."

"No, but I do in my old yard and so do the neighbors. I saw it as I was coming here. How are you fixed for water?"

"Got plenty in the garage."

I busied myself and got some of the plant leaves from next door and a fire going in his fire pit. I filled the cast iron pot he had on a three-legged iron stand and left it to boil. Then I pulled a cushion from the swinging couch and put it next to the fire so I could keep and eye on Kurt.

Lucky settled down and soon she was following me around. I took a quick look to see what he had growing. After the foxglove tea, I knew that I could make a nice vegetable soup with the fresh tomatoes, beans and garlic chives he had growing. He even had a small patch of corn and I pulled a couple of ears off to roast on the fire.

"Kurt, we need your help. We need to find water and learn about bees and growing crops. There are about a dozen of us in the foothills of North Vancouver," I swallowed hard. "We can start again, but it would be easier if we had help."

During the next few days I watched him and waited.

During these times I've seen amazing things and sometimes people will rally if they have a reason for going on. But it didn't happen. I was surprised; I would never have thought that Kurt would give up. Maybe his heart couldn't be helped with the simple tea we had.

I needed to make him realize how important he is to us.

"We'll take our time and you'll get stronger."

He looked me in the eyes and shook his head.

"Listen. You'll be fine. I have books. Take them, but please leave a note for the kids. They'll be home soon." His voice drifted off.

Me? Who was he kidding? I didn't know anything, not like he did. He had the knowledge and the practical experience. He was the valuable one.

I slowly realized that if Kurt was valuable with his old knowledge, maybe I was too? There wasn't anyone else but me to pass on the survival knowledge.

The thought terrified me.

I knew that I couldn't do it alone. I took a deep breath and felt a calmness and strength come over me.

A short while later he patted my hand as his eyes slowly closed and one last long sigh escaped from his lips.

I knew he was gone.

I cried for a long time. He was a good man and I didn't know what to do. It would take me hours to bury him and it seemed almost pointless with all the other dead in the city, but I didn't want the animals to get him.

I walked over to the beehive that he kept by the side of the garage with its partially caved in roof and looked at it. It was quiet. I waited for a few minutes to see if any bees would come out or go in. Not a bee in sight at the hive.

I had really hoped that Kurt would be able to help us. I didn't know what to do now. Grant and I were the oldest people in our group and we had very little experience with raising vegetables or fruit. But Kurt was a wise man and he seemed to think that I could do it. I would have to give it my all and I would.

I looked around the yard and found a long cement structure that was low to the ground. It was about four feet high and had a cement floor with an area for drainage. I realized that this must be the start of a new building or experiment that Kurt was doing, but I saw that this would be a perfect place for his body. I could use some of the metal roofing that had fallen down from his garage for its roof and then I could weigh it down with some heavy rubble to keep out the animals.

It took a while to get everything ready, but finally I went back to get Kurt's body. When I was finished I said a few words and a small prayer. I knew he would have liked that.

I was tired, very tired, bone tired. I sat down in the shade of the garage. Lucky came and sat a short distance from me and watched me. Books. Kurt said he had books. I knew that he would also have seeds that would help. I wouldn't be going home empty handed.

I slept for a long time. It was a very deep and restful sleep. As I woke I stretched my whole body from my fingers to my toes, it felt good.

The sun was warm on my face and a gentle breeze tickled my face. It was so relaxing with the sun, the breeze, and the drone of bees in the background. It was a lovely morning.

My eyes snapped open and I made sure that I didn't move.

Bees. I saw one slowly fly by me. Okay, they were bees, but were they the right kind? I got up and followed the little fellow to a small hive, about the size of a grapefruit between the branches of a tree a short distance from the old hive.

I carefully looked at the bees coming from the hive and then went to the old hive. They certainly looked the same.

71

I knew that if the old queen died the hive would move with a new queen. These bees had the same markings as the dead ones around the old hive so I knew that it was worth the risk and trouble of moving them.

Kurt had a small light, wide wooden cart in the back of the yard and I had seen that it was still there and seemed unharmed.

I emptied out the old hive of the little bodies, but kept the honeycomb. I hoped that the heat and lack of water when the comet hit had killed them, not some pre-Event virus.

I got the cart pulled up to the old hive and loaded it. I went to Kurt's green house that was covered with a light clear plastic tarp and looked in his garage and workshop. He had cleaned up and repaired a lot of the damage. I found books on topics that wouldn't be in modern libraries or bookstores.

I smiled to myself. These were books with basic old-time knowledge, written simply, beautifully illustrated and easy to follow.

I found a length of rope and managed to leash Lucky to the cart. She didn't take much persuading after I gave her a drink of water and some food. She was a docile female and a nice little girl despite the earlier growls.

I was very pleased to have a new companion and protector.

I wasn't sure how to move the little hive. Then I remembered that Kurt had bees shipped to him once in a small wooden box about the size of the old style matchboxes. I needed to find something that would let the air in, but would keep the bees contained.

I carefully went up the back stairs into the remains of the house. One side had completely collapsed, but the other side that had the chimney and the stairs to the basement and the second floor was still standing. I found a piece of cheesecloth in the basement that I hoped would do the trick.

Kurt's house had held up better than most of its neighbors after the earthquakes and fires.

The fire ravaged some area and left others untouched. Some blocks were completed blackened and flattened and others not so bad. A few small areas had a house or two that you might be able to live in, but there was nothing around and no sewage or electricity.

I loaded everything I could find that would be of use and would fit into the small cart. Lucky and I headed out the next morning at first light. I left a couple of notes for Kurt's children. That way if they ever did come home they would be able to find us.

There was still a lot at Kurt's place that we could use and a lot of information in the old-fashioned books I had to leave behind, but I could only take so much with me. When I got back, the group would have to decide whether or not someone should make this dangerous trip again. We would make that decision together.

I was pleased with what I was coming back with, but it didn't really solve the problem of water. We needed a sustainable water supply.

***

I entered the area below our cave site and looked up at the mountains. It did feel like I was coming home. It was amazing that in the few months after the Event sprigs of green were starting to break though the ground.

Fireweed. That's what would grow first and then other plants would follow. Good old mother earth would be fine.

It was getting to be dusk. I stopped to watch the western sky turn from the bight blue of the day to pink and purple. Were those wisps of cloud? Might the rain return?

I heard the children before I saw them and they came scrambling toward me asking for a story. I laughed at their excitement.

Then came Grant, with his arms wide open. He held me close and kissed me hard. I felt like my heart was going to break. I knew that I would have to make sure he did what we needed for the survival of people.

"I've missed you so much," he said through his tears. "Who do you have with you?" he asked to distract me as he looked at the dog.

Kent came up and gave me a quick hug too and took the cart.

"This is Lucky. She was with Kurt. He's dead. Buster died too. But I got bees, a hive, a whole bunch of seeds and books on all different topics. I'll tell you all about it," I said as we walked the rest of the way to camp.

"Good, you did really well. I was worried."

I nodded. I didn't really know what to say to him.

I walked into the camp and quickly kissed and hugged everyone. Then they left us alone so that we could have some time to ourselves.

We walked past the cave to a small flat rock. We sat in silence, just holding hands and looking at each other until it was so dark we couldn't see anymore.

"I've been thinking," he said.

I waited for him. I knew that this was going to be an important talk.

"I want you to trust me and I want to talk to you about two things. One is water. Do you remember the old stories Kurt used to tell, about his father finding water for the neighbors and how he did it a couple of times too?" Grant slipped a forked shaped tree branch into my hands. "I think it's willow, but I'm not sure."

"Oh, come on," I started to say and then stopped. I felt a strange light pull toward the ground when I slipped both my hands on the short sections of the branch. Strange, I'll have to take a closer look at it tomorrow it was worth further exploration. But not today, not when I could relax in Grant's arms for the first time in two weeks.

I could tell from his eyes that he was serious.

"The second is more important. You and me, I've been giving it a lot of thought and I think that I can help out and "do my duty" as they say, but still keep our commitment to each other. I think that we can accomplish both if we use some modern conveniences."

Now I noticed a bright glint in his eyes and a smile trying to break free around his mouth and he pulled out a turkey baster and handed it to me.

I looked at him speechless.

"You tell me that artificial insemination works really well for the birds and the bees. Well how about people? I know it's been done."

I started to laugh.

I knew that he was serious, but it was so ridiculous. It was also worth a try, both that and the dowsing were worth a try.

Just then I heard three little voices chanting louder and louder.

"Once upon a time. Once upon a time."

I knew that I was being called and I had to answer.

Grant and I went to the fire pit and found comfortable seats.

I began my story for the evening.

"Once upon a time there was a man named Kurt..."

A Little Old Fashioned

I sat in the long hall outside of the office of the man I was called to report to. It had drab light grey walls and dark brown speckled floor. The walls had large paintings from the old masters and they were as phony as the wooden bench I was sitting on. It smelt like disinfectant and stale sweat.

"Wanda Juliette Morgan." The pert and perky, blonde twenty something female receptionist for the Director of the Intergalactic Services Agencies (IGSA) called my name, "The Tribunal will see you now."

I took a deep breath, wiped my suddenly sweaty palms on my dark blue dress pants, stood up and followed as she led the way into the inner sanctum of the local big cheese of the General Alliance of Planets – GAP.

I just wanted this whole thing to be over, what was the worst they could do to me, give me a fine? Still I wondered how much it would be and if I was going to actually make and attempt to pay it off or just leave the planet and change my name.

I looked around at the Great Hall, the ceiling was white, and the walls were the same color as in the hallway, a light gray, and the floor a slate gray. So much for the use of color. I supposed that the use of heavy embossed cream silk on the walls and thick dark grey and burgundy wool carpets were to soften the effect.

I just wanted this mock disciplinary hearing to be over so that I can get to work and set up my homestead. Then I can explore Dora, my new home, a planet on the edge of the galaxy in the Centauri System.

So I lost a space ship, the Regal, and it's cargo. It's not the first time that's happened to the GAP. It was their fault that the coupling between the spacecraft and the cargo pod didn't hold and I had to jettison everything except for the emergency pod. It was the only way I could save myself. I was the Captain and the only crewmember since it was just a supply ship. Besides they have insurance, I thought as I entered the inner office.

It wasn't even the only time they had lost one of their supply ships.

I was the third one to run into trouble, One
had been completely destroyed and the other two one
Captain had turned back and the other had dropped the
cargo and run too.

"Before we begin the sentencing is there
anything the defense would like to say in the case of
Wanda Juliette Morgan versus General Alliance of
Planets?" the young personal receptionist, Miss Pert
said as she announced Wanda.

"Wait a minute. What's going on here?" I asked
as I was led to a seat behind a dark pine desk. I was
shocked. What was going on? I looked at Miss Pert
I thought that she was a receptionist why was she
acting like the head of the Tribunal? Even if they had
combined the jobs to economize this didn't make any
sense.

I tucked my short blonde hair behind my
ears and sat up straight trying to figure out what
was happening. I'd been told I would have a private
meeting with Director DuBuke. I felt my stomach start
to clench and the powdered eggs I had for breakfast
were starting the roll around my gut like marbles.
Something was definitely going wrong.

A small young man, with buckteeth, seated
next to me smiled. He started to stand and leaned over
to shake my hand.

"Preston, we don't have any time for all that. Just sit quiet and listen as we pass judgment," said a heavy set, jowly old man with a receding white hair.

That had to be Ross DuBuke, the head of GAP. They're the ones that had such bad equipment it's surprising anyone was left alive after their missions, I thought as I scanned the room.

It reminded me of the old Perry Mason, and Law and Order, historical vids my family loved to watch.

The room consisted of a long desk with three old folks in black robes seated on high back black chairs. Two shorter wooden tables with short black chairs faced them. I sat at one table beside Preston. At the other desk sat a very dapper man in his forties wearing a nice three-piece silver suit complete with a red power tie.

I had been ordered, I preferred the term, required, here today to talk about the mission and the equipment failure on board the Regal Queen, the ship I had flown to Darla and almost lost my life on.

What did they mean by sentencing? I'd been told this would be an informal disciplinary hearing. I would lose my commission, but would be able to keep the acres I'd been promised on Dora.

"Look, I've got a meeting in fifteen minutes so please let's just decide. Shall it be life in the hard labor colony of Lavinia, or death by hanging?" DuBuke smiled at Miss Pert who smiled back at him then left the room.

"What are you talking about? Labor colony or death?" I asked as I started to rise from my chair.

A big guy, a guard, I hadn't noticed before, because he was wearing gray to blend into the walls, pushed me down in my seat with his meaty hands and glared at me.

I stared at the three Tribunal members. They weren't smiling nor were they looking at me. They kept shuffling papers in front of them and looking everywhere else except at me.

I started to sweat and rubbed my hands down my pant legs. This wasn't going to be an easy "Oops, I'm sorry" situation. I surveyed the doors and windows looking for an alternate exit strategy.

I sensed the presence of someone watching me as the hair on the back of my neck began to rise. Goose pumps popped up on my arms and I shuddered.

My grandmother's old saying, "Someone must be walking over your grave," came to mind as I took a deep breath and slowly let it out.

I was terrified. I had the distinct impression that they were just sweeping everything under the carpet and throwing me out with the trash. It made sense, if I was gone, their record would be clean and there would be no one to say anything different.

The doors at the back of the room where I had come in suddenly opened and little Miss Pert came in almost running to DuBuke. Following her was a big ugly looking cowboy complete with a black Stetson. He looked like a giant steamroller. I don't think he would have stopped for anybody.

I looked at DuBuke saw him smile at Mr. Ugly as he nodded and accepted a file from Miss Pert. DuBuke opened the file and read it. His white busy eyebrows pulled together and his mouth puckered looking like he was sucking on a lemon, but as he looked up he forced himself to smile.

"Everyone out," said DuBuke in a loud gruff voice that echoed through the room. The gathered spectators and his fellow jurors jumped up and started to move as if the room was on fire. They scattered out the first available doors like scared rabbits.

I wanted to leave as well. I stood and turned to leave until I heard DuBuke's next words "Except, Ms. Morgan, my esteemed collogue and assistant" he said and I turned to look at him.

He smiled.

I knew that couldn't be something good. My knees were weak and I slowly sat down on my chair and watched DuBuke. I was cold, very cold it felt that my blood had turned to ice. I looked around, planning for an escape. I had decided that they weren't going to take me without a fight.

He spent a few minutes speaking with Mr. Ugly in hushed tones. Ugly's vacant beady-eyes fell on me; he pursed his lips and shook his head. DuBuke whispered a few more words to him, DuBuke's jaw was firm and his mouth a hard line, then a slow smile crossed his craggy face as Mr. Ugly sighed and nodded.

I knew I was in trouble, but it had to be better than hard labor or death right?

"Come here Ms. Morgan," said DuBuke in a slow solemn tome.

I glanced at the guard and watched him put one hand on the sidearm he was carrying. I didn't have a choice so I got up and slowly went to him.

Time was standing still, I was aware of everything the hum of the air conditioner and the soft movement of air on my face. The spongy give of the thick rug under my feet, the way my silk shirt felt against my skin and mostly how loud and hard my heart was beating in my chest.

"Yes, Mr. DuBuke?" I stood up straight and held my head high. As my granddaddy used to say, "No matter how afraid you are don't let them see you sweat". I slowly walked toward the two men until I stopped in front of his desk. I tried to look interested not terrified. My mouth was dry; it felt like it had been stuffed with sand.

"We have a little proposition for you. It's actually a very good one. It would be a really big help to all of us if you took it," he said smoothly as he steepled his hands together on the desk in front of him.

"I understand you want to stay and homestead on Dora?"

I nodded and kept quiet. I cleared my throat, swallowed. Maybe I would get another chance?

"Well, it just so happens we have a new opening at the Goodfriend Space Port. They're in need of a sheriff. And it seems you're very uniquely qualified for the position. I see in your file you of course are a space ships Captain and pilot, therefore a natural leader. You've also have experience in the Marine Corp as an MP, and some sort of secret elite force as well. Served with distinction, blah, blah, blah. Very impressive." He arched both eyebrows then pushed what I assume was my file toward his assistant. "If you want the job it's yours.

If you accept, your sentence will be expunged, and the land will remain yours too. What do you say?"

"Yes," was the only word I could croak out. What choice did I have? My land, a new start with a new job or death? Yes, I knew that it wasn't going to be as easy as it sounded and that it was going to be dangerous, but it was the chance of living free where I wanted to. It was worth the risk

"Excellent. Sign this," said DuBuke. He shoved the file toward me across the desk, opened it then handed me a pen.

I looked at the file and realized the only document in it was a very short contract saying that if I took on the job as Sheriff of Goodfriend Space Port all charges would be dropped, and I would receive the land I'd been promised.

I signed.

DuBuke, Pert and Ugly were all smiling at each other and at me. Mr. Ugly gave me such a hard pat on the back it almost sent me flying.

Miss Pert was fidgeting, moving from foot to foot, doing all she could not to bounce up and down and DuBuke's eyes kept shifting between her and me.

What every I had gotten myself in to? I knew it wasn't good, but I knew that this was better than the other options I was facing.

***

I arrived at Goodfriend Space Port accompanied by Mr. Ugly two days later.

When we got out of the helicopter I couldn't believe what I saw. Goodfriend was like walking into a 19th century frontier western town complete with wooden sidewalks, storefronts and houses. There were even buckboards and real horses.

The men in western gear were all dusty and dry looking. I looked at Mr. Ugly, whose real name was Mr. Cobb, he was wearing a full western outfit complete with Stetson and a holster with guns at his hip, he fit right in.

"Cobb, where are the women in this town? At a meeting or something?"

"No, we were expecting a shipment of women to come in on the big transport last week. We've been waiting for them for over a year now."

What are all these men going to do to me when they find out that I was the captain and pilot of that transport and that the cargo, all the female Sims were missing?

"You mean the big transport of Sims that was lost because of an equipment malfunction?" I asked struggling to keep my face straight and the knot of fear in my belly from my eyes. The mock trial was over but I still hadn't quite from defending myself. It was an equipment malfunction.

I soon realized this wasn't my worst problem. What are all these men going to do when they realize I'm the only woman in town?

As my mother used to say, "Oh Lordy, Lordy. What do I do now?"

"Yeah, well, I don't know anything about any equipment malfunction," Cobb said, "I just don't see the women we ordered. Who's going to mine the moon now? The male Sims were supposed to do that, now we don't have them. None of us are going up there I can tell you."

That answered my next question about the male Sims on the cargo manifest. The women were supposed to be companions to these men, and the males were suppose to take on the dangerous job of mining the moon for minerals to help line the pockets of the GAP.

Cobb told me they were going to blow up the moon to make it easier for the ships to land. I'm not sure he got all that right especially if they were getting money from the minerals on the moon.

Never mind how they were going to do it, the biggest questions would be why?

I remembered that there had been an ongoing protest at all the major cities on Earth about this moon. The local Dorians of course didn't want the moon disturbed, but they were offering concessions about mining it.

They just didn't want the moon destroyed. They were even willing to move it out of the direct path of Goodfriend. I thought this was really generous of them, although how they would move it I didn't know. It was beyond me.

I also heard about protests by the Sims about being used as companions. The Sims these days had full voting rights and were citizens of the country where they were manufactured. They were considered to be sentient beings under the law. They were self-aware and could reproduce with or without a partner. In the newest models you couldn't tell if they were manufactured or not. The biggest difference with the ones that were individually purchased you could have your memories transferred into your Sim. The corporate ones started to learn when they were activated, and when they started to develop their own personalities.

I think the entire debate was silly. The courts had even ruled on the subject.

But as far back as there have been humans, they always exploited the newest group that came into their territory. They tried to make them sub-human so they would be able to abuse them with a clear conscious.

"You're a woman aren't you?' said the clever Mr. Cobb, a new light shone in his little beady eyes.

I looked down at my pants, shirt, and fleece jacket then looked back at him and nodded. "Yes, Mr. Cobb, the last time I looked I was indeed a woman. At least that's what Mom and Dad told me."

I averted my eyes from him to take in more of this wonderful, dusty little town.

It seemed such a contradiction of worlds. The new like the helicopter we came in on, and the personal transports, and then others using horse drawn buggies.

Looking down the street I realized the closer you got to the center of town the more modern the street and buildings became. A few blocks away I could see smooth cement sidewalks and roads, and beyond I could see a few air-cars hovering between tall buildings.

But out here, on the outskirts of town, near the helipad, it was like the old west. I recalled from the history vids and the long dresses women wore in those days.

I always thought those dresses where designed to keep them from being too mobile and running away from the men.

I smiled at such a ridiculous thought.

"Mr. Cobb, I don't think that's a good idea. I think you're just too much of a man for me," I said with a straight face.

"But I saw you first."

"Yes, speaking of that first meeting, what is your position in this fair little town?"

"I'm the Mayor," he said with pride in his voice.

"So I'll be dealing with you directly. Good. Now I need to know where I'm going to live as sheriff, and more importantly where my land is located."

"Yeah, well I can get that information for you. Or at least I can show you to your office. Your secretary, Grant will give you a hand."

As we were talking, Cobb slung my suitcases and crate onto an automated lift then swung me up beside him. We held onto a handrail running from the front and the sides of the lift, the back was open.

After only a few blocks it appeared we had traveled a few hundred years back in time. The three and four story brick buildings were a mixture of apartment dwellings and commercial offices.

Cobb smiled at me; his small yellow teeth made me wonder if there was a dentist in this burg.

One thing I hadn't seen for sure were schools.

"Cobb, don't you have any schools?"

"No. No kids, no need for schools, or parks or church's for that matter. They're in the plans, but we were waiting for the transport with the Sims, ya know."

Okay, now I was starting to feel bad about the Sims on board the ship. Maybe they would have had an okay life here.

But for now none of this was my worry. I had to take care of my sheriff stuff so I could get my property and start to develop it.

Cobb stopped the lift in front of a charming three story red brick building. The lift settled onto the road and we got off.

On the front of the building was a sign that declared this to be the Goodfriend Space Port Police Department. There were heavy oak doors with glass inserts and a brass push bar Cobb led me through. I hurried after him.

"Here's your office, Sheriff." Cobb showed me into the inner office. The walls were painted a dull gray and matched the gray linoleum floor. The ceiling was an off white done in tiles.

There were pictures of planes, cars, rocket ships, and even a calendar depicting nude females hung on one of the walls. And a group of uniformed officers seated on hard back oak chairs.

"Listen up everyone. " said Cobb. This is our new sheriff. Her name is Sheriff Wanda Morgan. You got that?"

I watched the eight uniformed officers turn to stare at me. They each had a different reaction. For some their jaws dropped open, while others their eyes bugged out. A few pretended to be cool, as if a new sheriff arrived every day. I wondered if this might in fact be the case.

The only thing they had in common was their dark grey uniforms with light blue shirts, all crisp and pressed.

"Interesting decor," I smiled at Cobb and the uniformed officers gathered in the office to meet me.

I stood in front of the calendar and tipped my head one way then the other. To be fair they weren't completely nude, all the girls had something covering their naughty bits and pieces. Some had a piece of equipment or an accessory that the calendar was trying to sell strategically placed so not everything was out in the open.

"What's a matter, sheriff, don't you like our art work?" said a young little blond fellow who was trying to grow a mustache, but wasn't having much success with it.

There was a little snicker around the office from the guys.

I smiled and nodded.

"I guess art's in the eye of the beholder. But I'll tell you what, if you want to leave this up that's fair. But don't you come hollering to Mayor Cobb here when I do the same thing only with male nudes in my office."

I watched as the realization of my words sunk in to this group of men. They would have to look at naked guys whenever I called them into my office to review their reports and job performances, or any other meeting I might call. I'm certain they wouldn't enjoy having to look at men's bits and pieces on full display.

I saw one of the senior officers with three stripes on his shoulder lean over and take the nude calendar off the wall.

I caught his eye and smiled at him.

That was easy almost too easy. But I thought we were off to a good start. I believe in being an equal opportunity employer.

"And here is Grant Jones your personal assistant and right hand man. He just started with us a few days ago, but he's picking up really quick." Said the senior officer as he came over to me with the calendar in his hand.

In walked a man in his late thirties with short dark hair and deep brown eyes. He had a smile on his face that encouraged immediate trust.

My heart started to beat hard and my breath caught in my throat.

I took a minute to compose myself then nodded and smiled at Mr. Jones my new assistant, who was also my husband. He had been made the Chief Engineer on the Regal The Second when I had separated and jettisoned her.

My mind whirled with different questions. How and why was he here?

But my biggest question was where was the cargo from the Regal?

The last thing I knew I had left them in Grant's capable hands on the other side of the continent, where there was lots of fresh water and access to the ocean.

I couldn't talk to him now, not in front of everyone. My questions would have to wait.

A sharp cry from the street and the assembled officers rushed to the front door and opened it.

"Oh No!" came a broken cry from a young officer as the sounds of shots being fired from the street filled the office.

"The natives are attacking! We're surrounded," yelled one of the officers looking out the door before he tried to scramble back into the office. Before he was inside he was shot dead. He lay still in the open doorway in a pool of blood.

The smell of gunpowder and blood filled the room.

I heard shots coming from outside.

Those who hadn't made it outside froze in their tracks and turned to look at me. Their looks reminded me of a deer caught in headlights.

"Pull that man inside and close the door. And see if there is anything that we can do for him," I said adding the obvious.

"Grant. Cobb. Let's get some guns then come with me. The rest of you stay here and wait until you hear from me."

I followed Grant and Cobb to the gun locker where the three of us loaded up on rifles and ammunition. The weapons were new, yet old fashioned. I recalled a law banning energy weapons on the human outposts on the outer rim worlds.

The shots from the outside had stopped. I guess they were waiting for us to peek our heads out again.

"Captain, ah sorry, Sheriff. There is a back door," said Grant as he indicated with a nod of his head the coffee room in the back of the office. "There is also a way onto the roof from the third floor."

"Now that might work for us." I was trying to figure out which our next best move would be.

"Does anyone know why the Dorians are attacking?" I asked.

"Sure," Cobb shrugged. "They think we're going to start mining the moon."

"Ah yes, the mining and blowing up of their moon. Right. But that's not going to happen because the Sim workers weren't delivered right?" I asked Cobb.

"It's been put on hold until the next shipment arrives about a year from now," explained Cobb.

"Okay. Do we have to blow up their moon? I mean isn't that going to cause a lot of problems for this planet?"

"The natives have some mumbo jumbo belief that if the moon is destroyed it will mean the end of their world."

A large rock was shattered the window in the front door. There was a piece of white cloth wrapped around the rock. The Dorian's had sent us some mail.

I gazed at Grant and suppressed a smile. Someone had sent us a note. I retrieved the rock with the note attached.

"How many men have we lost?" My question was directed to both Cobb and Grant.

I could see Cobb's lips moving. I wasn't sure if he was counting the officers or was listing off their names.

"Two are missing," he finally reported.

I nodded in response as I unwrapped the white cloth from the rock.

"Bomb," said Grant as his arm shot out to stop me but I was too quick for him and had it off. Luckily it wasn't a bomb

It had been a very, very long time since I was in a situation like this and boy was I rusty. No one should have touched the rock until it was checked out.

I unfolded the large piece of plain white cloth and saw there was a note written in black ink on it.

"What does it say?" said the young blond policeman with the pre-pubescent moustache.

"They seem to want to meet with the Sheriff. But I really think the honor should go to you, Mayor Cobb," I said as I held out the note for him to take.

"Sorry, honey, I think they want to talk to the Sheriff and that's you," said Cobb smiling at me.

"Fine, I'll go, but first I want a minute to get myself ready in my office. Grant, you're with me," I said then led the way into my office.

I opened the office door and stepped in. I waited while Grant walked past me and closed the door. The office had glass windows on three sides, but there were blinds and I made sure they were closed so we would have some privacy.

I turned to Grant and found that he already had his arms around me. My lips found his as we quickly embraced. I knew there was no time, but it might be the last time we saw each other.

"I love you," Grant said as he looked into my eyes and smiled.

"I love you too and I have a lot of questions." I hugged Grant hard and then let him go. "I need a piece of paper and then ask one of the boys to come in here. Someone you can trust."

He gave me a sheet of blank paper I finished writing a quick note then slipped it into an envelope as Grant called to one of the officers.

A handsome middle-aged man walked into my office. I had noticed him before. He seemed the only calm one in the bunch. He hadn't run to get shot at when the Natives stormed us and opened fire. A cautious guy, not a runner-inner when danger required careful assessment. I liked that.

"I need you to witness my signature on my will. I also need you to swear on what you hold most dear that what you see you will not reveal to anyone."

The dark haired officer looked me in the eyes and then gave me a solemn nod. I signed the will and then handed the paper to him to sign as a witness. I wrote only to be opened upon my death, on the envelope and handed it to Grant.

With that taken care of I looked at the officer. "What's your name? And what do you think my chances are?"

"Buster. Pretty good," he shrugged his broad shoulders. "They could have come in here and killed us all if they wanted to. They have the numbers. I think they were firing at the doors and our fool officers got in the way of the bullets. They meant to get our attention not take our lives."

I had wondered that myself.

"Okay," I took a deep breath and looked at them.

"I'm headed out. Buster you take care of the men. Grant you've got my will make sure it stays safe and that you never have to open it." I said giving him a smile as I led the way out of my office.

***

I would have a quick meeting, maybe a couple of hours, and we would be done. But no.

The meetings went on for months.

During this time I heard evidence from the natives and the Members of the GAP about land claims and usage provisions. It seemed the two factions had been at loggerheads since the humans had come to this planet, and everyone's impatience had been growing. Neither side wanted to wait any longer. So when I arrived they thought I was the impartial judge they'd been waiting for to settle their disputes.

During this time I got to know the town and its people. And I could see the corporate angle of things too.

I also got a chance to look at the parcel of land that was deeded to me a few miles outside town.

The land was dry. The planet had water, but very little fresh water.

I went with the surveyors and the natives and had meetings with everyone about the land and the moon.

I spoke to the leader of Dorian's and once I had their starting point I went to DuBuke the leader of the GAP. He agreed to come to Dora so he would be there during the negotiations.

I watched him walk into my office. I never have stood much on ceremony and over the time I was here things had changed a little. I made sure that the windows and the door were left open.

I watched him study at my light salmon walls and dark chocolate floor, and the bright colorful artwork on the walls. Huge canvases of greens and yellows and orange and purple on one wall combined with photos on another wall of the starkness of wind swept hills and the scant rare trickle of water over smooth round rocks.

"OK, what have you got," were the first words out of his mouth.

"I've made a deal for you," I said as I smiled at him doing my best little woman impression for him. "I talked to the natives and I know you don't want them around the space port. I've almost got them talked into taking the western side of the continent.

With the Reckless Mountain Range being the dividing point for the Native colony and the local population. That would be good don't you think?"

I watched him hide a smile and then slowly start to shake his head. "I don't know. There's a lot of land there." His tone was hesitant. "We haven't really explored it all that well yet."

I nodded. "I was thinking too, although I know you've sent orbital surveyor's over it as well. Let's see here," I pretended to look at my notes then continued, "Oh, yes, there are I guess over a dozen homestead teams and they report the land is worthless. It seems to be really dry. No water anywhere."

DuBuke looked at me and started to smile. "Even if I give you the land what about the moon?"

"Yes, well, that is a problem. The natives want it left alone. They say if you agree they will move it out of the path of the Goodfriend, and if they can't they will never bring it up again."

I could see the greed oozing out of DuBuke's pores so I waited.

"I guess we might be able to accommodate the land deal. How did they say they were going to move the moon?" DuBuke looked at me his eyes had gone beady and hard.

I smiled and nodded at him as if sharing a joke and ignored the question.

I hadn't asked the Dorians on purpose. If I didn't know, then I couldn't tell anyone. To me it sounded too much like something the Powers that be would want to get their hands on. Something I didn't want to get involved with at all

"By the way, I took a look at the land you've given me to homestead and it's very generous being close to town and such, but I really did want to be out further. A lot further."

DuBuke sat still, the smile faded as he listened to me. I knew he knew the land he'd given me was less than worthless except for the scenery. It was high on the local mountain range with not a flat section of ground on the whole lot. He also knew that my Captain's contract had "a no responsibility" clause in it, one that I had insisted on and put in myself.

Now I know I'm a little old fashioned, but my mother always said, "Fool me once shame on you, fool my twice shame on me, try to fool me thrice and you'll pay the price."

DuBuke had his two times and I knew what kind of man he was.

He nodded uneasily. "What land did you want?"

"Do you remember that peninsula where the cargo section of the Regal crashed? I'd like to take that off your hands. I also plan on resigning, effective immediately. If you sign that property over to me now I'll consider our bargain concluded." I kept my shoulders loose and my hands at my side. I know that I had a slight polite smile on my face and my eyes were clear and open. Mentally I was planning the next painting I was going to do right after this meeting.

DuBuke smiled tightly at me and stood up. He held out his hand and shook mine and turned to leave. "Certainly. I agree with your resignation and the land you have identified is now your property"

"Before you go, do you have the authority to sign on what we just talked about? Let's make this a real reason to celebrate and sign the land documents right now. I have them drawn up just like we've discussed. What do you say?"

I pulled out a short sheaf of papers and motioned for him to sit down again. I knew that he did have the authority to sign and was prepared.

He sat down in the chair across my desk then took a moment to quick scan the papers. He looked up at me his mouth curled in a big old-fashioned grin. "Where do I sign?" he asked.

"I'll get a good pen." I stood and leaned out my open office door. "Buster, would you bring me a proper pen please?"

Buster was waiting and ready so he appeared with a pen in hand. "Here you go, sir," he said as he handed the pen to DuBuke.

Dubuke looked at him, nodded then turned to sign his name on the documents. The pen was special it recorded his fingerprints and the date.

"Thank you," I said as I took the pen from him and signed the documents too. I smiled a very satisfied smile.

"It doesn't mean anything, you stupid girl. It has to be witnessed by two individuals," he said as stood to leave shaking his head.

"Oh, yes, those little technicalities. Simon could you come in please?" I said as I handed the pen to Buster as he signed and then another senior officer who had been waiting standing just outside the door, with a clear view of the process came in to sign as well.

"I have power of attorney, filed with our Mayor this afternoon, on behalf of the Dorians representing them for their land claims."

I thought DuBuke was going to have a heart attack. His face became as red as fresh beets and he started to gasp for air.

I waited for him to calm down.

"Yes, but we have the moon. The stupid fools."

"Actually, if you look for the moon this evening you may be surprised, it will be slowly moving to it's new orbit. It's something they do every five thousand years. It helps realign the gravitational Ley lines of the planet. Which also affects the energy and water flow of the planet. You'll find things quite different in the morning."

I smiled to myself. Tomorrow I would go home to my little homestead with Grant, my husband. It would be good to see what my friends and fellow Sims have accomplished in the last few months on the peninsula we had homesteaded.

I was one of the really lucky ones, a lot of me was new, but I was still a little old fashioned.

One Day At A Time

Ellen stood wearing her purple fleece night gown on her long, wide back deck facing the Inlet with a steaming cup of coffee in her hand looking out at the water.

It was such a mild morning on the Sunshine Coast on this first week of January, she couldn't believe how fortunate they were this year. It seemed that they had escaped any snow at all.

Only a few cold days of below freezing at night, just enough to set her spring flowering blubs was all they'd had. She looked over at the side yard at the buds on her magnolia that were swelling and the roses that she had planted last summer, they were still in bloom only four weeks ago.

Then her eyes glanced at the lads, their dogs, playing tag in the back yard. One Samson, a seven-year-old golden retriever and the other a small fourteen year-old red terrier, Rusty.

Rita Schulz

The heavy rains they had for the last two week had stopped so today would be a good day to stretch their legs, they all needed a walk.

She looked back out at the water, she never tired of looking at the keyhole view they had of the Georgia Straight, the stretch of water between themselves and Vancouver Island. A well-seasoned sailboat captain had told her that there were only about eight miles of water between Gibsons and the large Vancouver Island. All she knew was when she and Lee, her husband of twenty-five years had seen this little two story home with it's level entry and walk out basement they knew they had found home.

There was lots of room for family and guests and the tall evergreen and arbutus trees that surrounded it made if feel cozy, their little cabin in the woods.

As she watched the water, she realized that something was wrong. In all the time they had lived here you could get to the water by walking a long set of wooden stairs.

Kelly leaned over the railing and looked at the waves between the trees on the right side of her view. The waves were coming from the west usually that meant fair weather, but something stank, really, badly.

It wasn't the pulp mill, they got the odd smell from there a couple of times a year.

No, this was like Oyster Bay at very low tide, mud, dead shellfish, oysters, muscles and seaweed. It made you want to heave.

She had never, ever no matter how low the tide got had seen the bottom. There was always water covering the rocks and gravel directly below them, but not this morning.

She'd left the television on when she checked the weather station and now she heard the emergency signal. At least that's what she thought it was. She called to the dogs as she went back into the house and looked at the large television in the corner of the living room between the bay window and the built in mantel over the wood-burning fireplace.

She heard Matthew her three-year-old grandson getting up and coming into the living room and gave him a quick smile. "Honey, why don't you go and find Grandpa? Tell him I want to see him right now. Hurry please," she said. She tried to emphasize the words without scaring Matthew. The boy scooted away as the announcer came on.

"A comet hit the Pacific ocean this morning. We are expecting earth quakes in the next few minutes and tidal waves to batter the Pacific Northwest this late morning, especially the area from San Francisco to Canada," said a man who could barley contain his fear.

Ellen quickly turned off the television in case Mathew heard what was happening. She looked to the telephone should she try and call Mathew's parents? She had to at least try. Then she'd make a quick call to her other son too. She picked up the cordless phone and started to dial. All she got was a busy signal even before she finished the phone number. She put it down on the kitchen counter.

Oh God, please not that.

She had heard so much about tsunamis from her friends in Oregon, all she could do is repeat what they had said to her over and over again. Get to higher ground. Get to higher ground. It was litany that kept repeating in her head. Kelly felt herself start to panic and then her rational brain kicked in. You can panic later, but right now you need to act.

"Lee, I need you to come up right now! I mean right now!" she called down to the basement. She hoped he heard her, he had to come now.

They had at most five minutes to leave and get to higher ground. She checked her watch. Okay go.

Once the earthquakes started there was no telling how the road around her would hold up and they had to get out before the tidal wave.

What do you need? And I mean need? She thought the herself as she went through her list of must have things.

She ran into the guest bedroom and grabbed a large wheeled backpack. She was like a mad woman as she ran through the house opening drawers. Grabbing three of for each of them, three socks and underwear, three tee shirts, three pants, running shoes and hiking boots. She grabbed the dog bowls, their kibble, luckily they had just gotten more the other day and their treats.

They had to get out of here. Don't dawdle she thought as she ran into the living room and grabbed the photos and albums off the mantel and the antique oak mirrored hutch.

The best place would be the Safeway parking lot at the junction of Pratt and Gibsons Road. It was very high ground and she knew that this whole area was on a massive granite vein of rock that stretched for about fifty to one hundred miles all down the coast.

112

The dogs came bounding into the house, barking, happy to be able to play without the benefit of the dark days and heavy rains that they had been having, which was typical of a winter in Gibsons.

She ran and slammed closed the sliding glass patio door so the dogs couldn't get out.

"Lee, I need you here right now!" Kelly yelled all pretense of niceness gone. She tried to weight her odds of how many people would be trying to get to Safeway to find safety and food and water.

She heard the basement door open and Mathew's light little boy's voice chatting to his grandfather as they came up the stairs.

"What's the problem Ellen? We're coming," he said as he walked up the stairs with her budging laptop bag in his hand. He looked over the banister and saw her dragging the case with their clothes to the front door.

He took one look at her and quickly walked to her side and put an arm around her. "What is it, one of the kids?" he asked softly in her ear.

"No, worse, much worse. A comet has hit the Pacific Ocean, there's going to be tidal waves and earthquakes.

There talking like the San Andrade's Fault
it finally going to let loose too," said Ellen as she
watched Lee's eyes got softer as she spoke so fast
most people would not be able to understand her.
Then he looked around the foyer and by the front
door, licked his lips and nodded.

"I know. I've got my lap-top and the mini
tower," he said a as he walked into their pantry, pulled
out a large cloth shopping bag went down the hall and
pulled down three of his favorite paintings that she
had done over the years.

"We need to get to higher ground right now,"
they said in unison.

"They said they don't know when things are
going to happen but I figure we've got five minutes.
Listen carefully," she said looking at her wristwatch.
"We've used three of the already.

She quickly went through the things she had
packed from flashlights with extra batteries to toilet
paper and everything in between. He listened as
she spoke and they started to carry things to the tan
colored RAV4 they would be taking with them.

"Can you think of anything else? I don't
have fresh water so I used some of our buckets and a
couple of pots with tap water. I'm hoping to get some
more water at the grocery store,"

Ellen had to stop for a minute, she was breathing so hard and her mouth was so dry she was starting to get dizzy.

Lee put his arms around her and held her in his arms. "It's going to be okay. We have Vancouver Island to take the brunt off the tidal action and as for earth quakes as you told me when we bought the house the huge granite vein under us and Mt. Capstone behind us has stood for many years and will be here for a very long time to come. We'll see how the house and your Studio do," he laughed softly as he gently pushed her short dark brown hair from her face and kissed her forehead.

They looked at each other nodded and quickly pulled the rest of the things out of the front door and into the back of the Rave.

In Ellen's head she kept on hearing, *get to higher ground, get to higher ground.* "We are, we are," she mumbled under her breath to herself.

Lee and Ellen picked up Mathew, strapped him into his car seat in the back seat and then Ellen armed with a pocket full of dog treats grabbed Rusty and threw him in the rear foot well with a treat then grabbed Samson and put him the back seat too.

As she was going to close the back door, Mathew started to cry and kick his feet.

"It's okay Mathew, we're going on a car ride up to Safeway, " she said as she leaned forward and pick up a toy that had fallen onto the seat, as she did Samson decided that he would squeeze past her and he started to head up the driveway.

Ellen's heart almost stopped. She knew that Samson had been really bad lately about coming when called. She could feel her stomach clench and her mind jumped to 'what might happen'.

She had to get him in the car now. They had to leave NOW! T

hey had to get to hire ground. Above all else they had to keep Mathew safe. And that might mean leaving Samson behind. She felt her eyes swell with tears and her vision blurred. She prepared herself, she'd have to live with whatever happened.

She only had one chance before they left.

"Okay, Sampson. Come," she said with authority.

Sampson walked to the top of the driveway and sniffed their hedge. She shook the dog treats. "Sampson. Cookie."

The dog looked up at her and slowly wagged his tail, his tongue lolled out from the side of his mouth. Great the dog was grinning at her thinking it was a game.

She felt Rusty jump up onto the back seat of the RAV. "Sampson, car ride. Cookie."

In her heart Ellen was begging for Sampson to come. She turned her back to the dog, shook the bad of treats and gave Rusty another cookie making sure that Sampson could see what she was doing. "Please God, please," she whispered under her breath, begging for the big dog to come.

"Get in the truck Ellen. He's wondering down the street," said Lee in a resigned, but firm voice.

She knew that she could just walk up to him and get him, but he was wandering to far away now. He'd gone a block and a half and they only had a few precious moments. She couldn't risk all their lives.

She closed the rear door and quickly walked around the truck and slid into the front passenger seat. She held back the tears, she would never forgive herself for leaving Samson, her big goofy buddy. She could feel sobs fill her chest and tears fill her eyes, she looked out of the window and tried to swallow her grief.

Maybe they would find him after this was all over. He knew the area because of their walks together, and he was smart. She bet that he'd get home before they would, but her tears wouldn't stop.

"Okay let's go!" she said as she put on her seatbelt and slammed the door closed. She took a deep breath and held onto the armrest.

Lee stepped on the gas, nothing happened. Lee tried again, but the car wouldn't start. Nothing. This had never happened to her before. He looked at Ellen. She glanced at him as she opened her door and jumped out.

"It won't start. Look grab Mathew and start up Third Street I'll meet you at Safeway or along the road," said Lee as he looked at Ellen.

She almost laughed at the suggestion. Yea, she could get a short way up the hill, but not all the way to the highway, but it was a good four to five miles away. Would she get there with a small three-year-old boy in tow in the next few minutes. Not a chance.

"Come on get out. I'll get the car going," she said. She stood to the side and Lee jumped out. She slid behind the wheel, waved her remote control key, stepped on the brake firmly, and then hit the start button once it went green.

A welcoming deep rumble greeted their ears as the car sprang to life.

"Okay, let's try this again," said Ellen and she got into her seat.

She looked up and noticed that the steady traffic in front of their door had slowed and then stopped.

"Lee, let's go up Third and then swing up Robin. I have a feeling that the traffic is plugged on Ocean View. Besides we'll constantly be going up and getting higher," said Ellen as she cleared her throat.

Lee checked the radio, there was only static on all the stations twice and nothing was on any of them, he turned it off.

"Gram, breakfast?" asked Mathew who had been very quiet up to now.

"Sure how about a nice soft blueberry bar and some water?" Ellen asked as she pulled up the large bag of snacks, juice and their small amount of bottled water. She opened a bar and handed it to him.

Ellen, rolled down her window, everything was eerily quiet. No bird song, no chitterling from squirrels, no eagles cry. She looked up, no birds, the only thing moving were the trees swaying with the wind.

"We'll go as far as we can. The Safeway lot is probably full right now. Any ideas?" asked Lee as he kept the truck steadily moving.

Suddenly the truck started to sway. A huge sixty foot maple tree in front of them started to lean and then fall. The crash shook the truck luckily it fell away from the road. Lee stopped and waited. There were only a few cars before and behind them, they all stopped as well. They continued crawling forward and arrived at the corner of Overlook and Proud and turned left. They had passed by the steep switchbacks and the s-curves on Overlook now the road was straight all the way up to the main highway, where the Safeway was.

They drove up Proud slowly there were cars and trucks in the ditch, people walking up the road carrying children and belongings. They would occasionally look behind them at the water then back toward the mountain where they were heading.

They were about a mile away from the Safeway when another earthquake hit, this time the telephone poles across the street started to fall like dominoes along the road and not across it, they kept on moving. So far so good.

"I don't think that we'll have much of a problem here in Gibsons. At least not at first. The house may even be standing.

"It probably won't have any glass windows left, and we won't have electricity, but I'm hoping that we still have a working septic tank, but I guess we need electricity for that, don't we?"

Lee nodded as he watched the road and the other cars around him waiting for another quake to hit them.

"I am worried about the kids, and our family and friends in Vancouver. I think some places will be fine. Don't you?"

"I know, I'm worried too. Look out the window, can you see the ocean from here? Maybe it won't be as bad as they predict. I'm worried about the ferries," said Lee letting Ellen's question hang.

Ellen craned her head toward the water. "I don't see any... oh, now I see water. It's about half way across to the Island. I can't see what's happening on the other side of the Island in the Long Beach area. I sure hope they get clear of all this. Mathew's asleep."

Lee nodded as they were buffeted again, this time harder and the truck slid to the right. He stopped, waited, and then proceeded slowly.

"Sason. Sason, where is he?" asked a sleepy Mathew as he woke and stretched. He started to sniffle as he looked around.

"I want Sason. Here Sason!"

Ellen looked at Lee and saw tears in his eyes that he brushed away with the back of his hand. She swallowed hard trying to keep herself from getting emotional. "What do I say? How do I tell him that we just left Samson?"

"No. It's like we said, Samson went for a walk, he's exploring and we hope he's at home by the time we get back."

Ellen nodded and used her fingers to the rub the tears from her eyes. She felt like such a failure. She should have done something, she should have trained the dog better. But if that dog, no, when that dog came back he would be so trained no one would recognize him. She'd make sure of it.

"Honey, Samson went exploring, remember? Hopefully he'll be finished and at home when we get there. Do you want some water now? She reached back and unscrewed the bottle. Remember only a little bit at a time."

The little boy took the bottle and she grabbed a towel and put it on his chest in case he spilt. She watched him and smiled. He was their reason to continue on. They had to protect him and make sure that he didn't just survive but that he thrived.

He was the reason they had to go to higher ground, he was the reason they would be alright.

"I was thinking of somewhere else that we could go, in the same area? Ideas?"

"How about George's place. You remember the contractor that built the studio and the fences for us?"

"Yea? Oh, the empty lot or lots in his subdivision?" asked Lee. He smiled and nodded at Ellen.

"Yea. If the empty lots are full of cars, maybe we can park on the street. At least for tonight? We're high enough now," said Ellen looking back over her shoulder.

"Okay."

"I also um… have a shovel if we need to dig a hole. It will be just like camping when the kids were little, won't it?" Ellen looked at him and grinned, she remembered how much he hated camping.

"Honey, I'm afraid that we're going to have to take this one day at a time and hope for the best."

She was concerned over a lot of things, would they have water, would they have electricity, would they have help from the mainland. How many people would likely die without their medication, could they get it?

How many would be gone in the next three weeks, three months, six months or a year?

Ellen stopped the racing thoughts in her mind, she had to focus on what was happening right now and deal with the problems and solutions in front of them.

She knew there were people that lived off the grid here on the Sunshine Coast so if they had to face this crisis this was a good place to be. Only time would tell but right now she had to calm her mind about the what-ifs.

They reached the cross roads of the main highway and drove to the other side.

Ellen felt herself relax. They were well over the tsunami level now.

"Keep driving, I see that the Safeway is full, but I still see empty lots in George's subdivision. We're going to be okay, at least for today," Ellen said as she reached over and squeezed Lee's hand.

All they could do was do their best, and as Lee said, take it one day at a time.

About the Author

Rita Schulz lives ion the Sunshine Coast of British Columbia. with Russ, her husband who is also a fiction writer.

She loves to read and paint in her spare time. She is learning to enjoy golf, and he is learning to enjoy gardening. They are kept company, and on track, by their two dogs and Glenn, their younger son.

She has written for years and is an alumni of the Oregon Writers Network and the Greater Vancouver Chapter, Romance Writers of America. To find out more about her and her work visit her website at http://www.ritacrossley.com

Also by Rita Schulz

Short Fiction

Blarney
Flower & Bird
Party Central
Once Upon a Time
The Scarlet Curse
Spoken Words
The Brownie's Holiday
A Little Old Fashioned
In The Land of Dragons
A Little Kitchen Magic
Silver Light
For Pete's Sake
Cleaning Up is Hard to Do
Confessions of a Bold Maiden
All for One
Lucky List
A Spark of Courage
Party Line
Spoken Words
Spirit Inn
One For All
Graybill
Rebellion
The Prize

Collections

Ladies of the Jolly Roger with Russ Crossley
Ten Tempting Tales with R.S. Meger
The Fantastic Five with R.S. Meger
Unique Tales of the Fantastic
Tales of the Fantastic
Nightmares
The Reckoning
The Dark Zone
Collage (coming soon)

Novels
Fire In Their Hearts with Russ Crossley

Also available from 53rd Street Publishing.

Nightmares come in many forms and from many places.

Blood thirsty vampires.
Flesh ripping werewolves.
Brain eating zombies.
Spirits of the dead who walk among us.
Monsters of unspeakable horror appearing from the darkness.

They attack us from the past.
They attack us from alternate realities,
They appear from the depths of unspeakable
darkness thirsting on our fear.

These tales of terror are guaranteed to keep you awake at night with the lights on. So sit back keep the lights burning brightly and hope there isn't a power outage.

Check out other exciting titles at http://www.53rdstreetpublishing.com